Shelter Bay

Pamela S. Meyers

Published by Scrivenings Press LLC
15 Lucky Lane
Morrilton, Arkansas 72110
https://ScriveningsPress.com

Printed in the United States of America

Paperback ISBN 978-1-64917-016-3

eBook ISBN 978-1-64917-017-0

Library of Congress Control Number: 2020940052

Cover by Diane Turpin, www.dianeturpindesigns.com

(Note: This book was previously published by Mantle Rock Publishing LLC and was re-published when MRP was acquired by Scrivenings Press LLC in 2020.)

All characters are fictional, and any resemblance to real people, either factional or historical, is purely coincidental.

Scriptures marked NKJV are taken from the NEW KING JAMES VERSION (NKJV): Scripture taken from the NEW KING JAMES VERSION®. Copyright© 1982 by Thomas Nelson, Inc. Used by permission. All rights reserved.

All other scriptures are taken from the KING JAMES VERSION (KJV): KING JAMES VERSION, public domain.

For the Geneva Lake Museum, whose staff members dedicate themselves to preserving the history of the Geneva Lake area educating all who come about the area's deep historical roots. Thank you for making the GLM a valuable resource for me and all the authors who love to set their historicals in our beautiful area.

ACKNOWLEDGMENTS

It's been said that it takes a village to raise a child. But I'm here to say that it takes a village to write a historical novel set in a real place. One might think because I grew up in Lake Geneva, Wisconsin there would be little to research because I already know everything about the town and lake. Nothing could be further from the truth.

Without the Lake Geneva Library and its collection of historical writings and microfilms of the weekly newspaper editions published during the time of my stories, I could never have learned as much as I have. I knew some of the history behind the many beautiful estates that make up much of the shoreline of Geneva Lake since the Great Chicago Fire in 1871, but I didn't know much about the people who built those homes or the can-do spirit of the town's early pioneers.

The Geneva Lake Museum, to whom I've dedicated this book, has also been a wonderful resource for me. From pictures of what 1893 Lake Geneva looked like, to displays of clothing from that era and actual buggies from the 1800s on display, and more. Thank you for being there GLM!

I also want to say a special thanks to Chris Brookes who is a

Lake Geneva history nerd like me, for the wonderful book on the steamboats of Geneva Lake. I was able to use a lot of what is talked about in the book, including mentions of some of the boat builders like Mate and his most unusual beard. Yes, he really did style his beard that way.

I can never write an acknowledgement page without saying thank you to my life group ladies from my church. Betty, Sue, Judy, and Fran, your prayers getting me through the plotting, writing and deadlines are what has sustained me.

Thanks also to my editor and publisher, Kathy Cretsinger. I so appreciate your input and encouragement!

Last, but certainly never least, I thank my Lord and Savior, Jesus Christ, whom I try to glorify in every story I write. He is the one who called me to this writing gig and equipped me with the skills and desire to write.

There is one more story to come in this Newport of the West Series, then after that, I'm not sure what story will emerge in my thoughts. But one thing you can be sure of. My stories will always highlight my Wisconsin roots.

Charm is deceitful and beauty is passing,
*But a woman who fears the L*ORD*, she shall be praised.*
Proverbs 31: 10 (NKJV)

CHAPTER ONE

Lake Geneva, Wisconsin - August 1893

The backdoor to the alley opened and a gust of warm humid air ruffled the receipts strewn across Maureen Quinn's desk. She dropped a multicolored glass paperweight on the papers and turned to see Leonidas Fitzsimmons' grizzled countenance twisted into his trademark snarl, appearing the same in death as it had in life.

"Sorry about that, Mo. The wind out there is fierce. Jimmy Owen replaced the tarp that had covered the old man's face, but not before the grotesque image had been seared into her mind.

She swallowed the sour taste that always appeared at times like this and turned away, keeping her focus on the accounting register in front of her. Her parents had warned her when she applied for the bookkeeping job that Nimrod Owen and Son was more than a furniture store. Something she already knew, since Mr. Owen was also Lake Geneva's one and only undertaker. Da had also reminded her how she'd refused to step into the parlor where they'd placed Granny's open casket. Instead, she'd listened to the funeral service from the adjacent living room. She didn't know what was worse. Seeing Granny so life-less or the cloying scent of gardenias and roses permeating the room.

Being the daughter of a florist, you would think she'd be accustomed to the blending of fragrances. But that smell was nothing when compared with the sweet and sickly odor from the embalming fluids that often seeped up the stairs and triggered a monster of a headache. It was time to find a new job.

The door slammed, indicating everyone was inside. "Just tell me when you get him downstairs and I'm free to turn around." She and her father were going to have a talk tonight. No matter that Mr. Owen gave the flower shop a lot of business.

"You can turn around now, Mo." At Jimmy's shout from the cellar, Maureen stood and stepped into the furniture shop at the front of the building. She weaved between a pair of coffins, one an expensive oak and the other pine.

The furniture business was slow today with only one custom lounge sold to a newcomer to the lakeshore. The promised opportunity to sell furniture on occasion had never materialized for her but once, when Mr. Owen and Jimmy had to both be away. Not that she aspired to sell furniture for the rest of her life. She sighed. Truth was, she had no idea what she should do next.

A part of her yearned to be independent and adventuresome, but another part desired to raise a family with a husband who adored her at least half as much as Da loved her mother. So far, she'd only known one man who could be the answer to the dream, but Preston Stevens had his own troubles and was in no position to consider marriage. Besides, he only thought of her as a pal. Same as they'd always been since they were toddlers.

She crossed to the large front window. The landau carriage belonging to Mrs. Ripley who lived in the large home on Baker Street passed by. Only James, Mrs. Ripley's driver, was on board. Maureen had been told her mama had lived in Mrs.

Ripley's house for a short time after the great fire when the home was owned by Jerusha Maxwell, the widow of one of the town's founding fathers.

Da came right behind the Ripley carriage, driving his wagon with colorful flowers painted on its side, likely making a delivery. She stepped back to avoid his seeing her. She'd see him soon enough this evening and he wasn't going to like what she had to say.

Later that afternoon, Maureen dropped the bag containing her skirt into the basket attached to her bicycle's handlebars, then swung her leg over the center bar and settled onto the seat. She took in a deep breath and silently thanked Amelia Jenks Bloomer for popularizing the puffy billowing pants that bore her name and allowed her to protect her modesty. She enjoyed wearing a pretty dress as much as the next woman, but there were times when such attire just wasn't practical. Like riding a bicycle or playing tennis or solving cases as a private detective.

She laughed at the final thought. Ever since she'd heard about Pinkerton agent Kate Warne's work as a detective, the adventuresome part of her had secretly dreamed of becoming one herself. If she remained in small town Lake Geneva her desire would never be fulfilled. It was a wild idea, but a few more months of saving from the pittance she was paid for keeping Mr. Owen's books and she'd be on her way to the city.

The backdoor to the store opened and Jimmy stepped out. He hitched up his pants that his suspenders regularly failed to keep in place, given his slender frame. "You be careful on that wheel, Maureen. We want you back here tomorrow and not hear you've ended up at the infirmary."

She laughed. "I'm always careful, Jimmy. You know that."

He grinned. "The day you're careful on that contraption I'll be an old man. See you tomorrow—I hope."

She gave a wave then started toward Geneva Lake where she'd take the shore path toward the Safe Refuge estate, the only home she'd known all of her twenty-two years. She lifted her face to the sun, thankful the heatwave they'd had the past week had broken. If she had a penny for every time she'd heard warnings from Mama she should never let the sun touch her skin, she'd be a rich woman.

It was bad enough women were expected to wear so many layers no matter how warm the day. And to have to always wear a hat. It was just plain nonsense. Those were rules she had no trouble breaking. As she picked up speed to cross Broad Street, the puffy sleeves of her shirtwaist blouse billowed out like tiny parachutes. Maybe the wind could lift her. She extended her arms and tilted them as she'd seen birds do in the air. Closing her eyes, she slanted to the right and laughed at the sensation of flying.

The bicycle tipped and she grabbed the handlebars, but the wobbling front wheel had rolled into a wagon wheel rut. She pedaled harder, but it was too late. Her face hit the dirt and her body scraped across the muddy road, stopping short of a pile of horse manure.

Maureen lifted her head and spit out a mouthful of dirt. One day she'd figure out how to fly but not today. She wiggled her extremities and assured of no broken bones, she sat up and brushed dirt off her torn blouse. Her bloomers appeared intact but were caked with mud. She peered through the tear on one of the mutton sleeves. If her only injury outside of her dignity was a scraped arm she'd manage.

The bicycle's back wheel was where it belonged, but where was the front wheel? She spotted it back where her failed attempt to fly began. Now to figure out how she was going to get home and where to hide the bicycle parts until she could get them put back together.

"Maureen, are you all right?"

The deep baritone voice that always set her stomach to fluttering broke into her thoughts. She turned and spit out a mouthful of dirt. "Preston Stevens, you always pick the worst times to bump into me."

He chuckled. "Whenever I have a chance to rescue my favorite girl, it's a good time." He hunched down and came to eye level with her. Using his thumb and index finger, he flicked something off her cheek. "You really took a tumble. When will you learn to be more careful?"

She drew in a breath and willed her fluttering stomach to settle. "When have you known me to ever be careful? And you should talk, Mr. Daredevil."

He chuckled. "When did you get the bicycle?"

"A few weeks ago. I've been riding it to and from work."

"Looked to me like you were attempting to turn it into a flying machine."

Her face heated. "You saw that?"

The creases around his intense blue eyes deepened. "I was rooting for you, Mo. I've no doubt that if you could fly, you would."

He understood her like no one else, which was why he was the perfect man for her. He just needed to learn how to rein in the desire to buck against all the rules and choose wisely which ones needed to be adhered to. As if she should talk. She moved to stand and pain shot up her left leg. She sat back down."

He gripped her arm. "Let's try again. Use my arm for support."

He eased her to her feet. "How do you feel now?"

Grateful to be able to lean on his shoulder, she said. "I've felt better. I'm sure I'll be fine and able to walk home in a few minutes."

"No need for that. I've got the *Ida* hitched to the city dock. I'll take you."

Relief washed over her. She may have sounded brave, but truth be told she wasn't sure if she could walk the distance to

Safe Refuge. The shore path was well worn from use, but one had to keep an eye out for gopher holes and stray rocks.

Still keeping hold of her arm with one hand and using his other hand, Preston grabbed up the main body of her bicycle, her bag still sitting it its basket. He studied it a moment. "The frame is bent, but it should be fixable. Let's get you out of the road. Are you able to grab the front wheel?" He wrapped his left arm around her waist. "Lean on me and take your time."

With his help she secured the front wheel under her arm by threading her hand between the spokes and, using her other arm, she leaned on him as they walked toward the docks a short distance away.

"You still doing okay, Mo? We can stop and rest a minute."

"I'm fine, but what are people going to think? Me with my torn blouse and mud caked face, leaning on you while you carry my bent bicycle? I'm afraid my reputation in this town just went down another notch."

He uttered a low chuckle. "Is this the same Maureen Quinn I've known since we were in diapers who never gave a fig what others think?"

"I know. It's shocking me as well. I'm thinking more of you. Ever since you arrived home, tongues have been wagging about your getting kicked out of Yale."

"And my dad never lets me forget it. Maybe by showing my chivalrous side by helping you my standing will be enhanced. You know, as always I'm grateful for your support, Mo."

They stopped next to the *Ida*, the small steamboat the Stevens family owned. While Maureen leaned on a piling, Preston jumped onto the boat's deck and set the bicycle's twisted body on the polished wood floor. "Let's get you onboard next."

She gripped both his outstretched hands and gingerly placed her right foot on the deck, grateful for the calm waters and the strength of his arms. She then eased the left foot across the short distance from the dock to the deck and put weight on it. Her knee gave out and she tumbled against Preston's hard chest. He two-stepped back and fell against the wooden box that covered the vessel's boiler, Maureen landing on top of him.

He held his arms out, obviously in an effort to not give anyone watching the wrong idea, and, despite the pain radiating from her left knee down to her ankle, she scrambled to an upright position.

He came to his feet and rearranged his jacket then scanned her length. "You okay?"

She nodded and hobbled to one of the wooden chairs arranged on the deck. "I'm fine."

"Good." He hopped onto the pier, grabbed the bike's front wheel then released the boat's rope from the piling and jumped onto the boat deck. "Next stop, Safe Refuge."

Within minutes he had the vessel backing away from the dock. The warm August air, slightly cooled from traveling over the water, felt good on Maureen's face. She glanced off, noticing he was staying close to the shore for the short trip.

Just past the ice company, the shoreline curved southwest and passed Linden Lodge, a large three-story home. As a child, Maureen loved watching the blades of a large windmill, sitting a short distance from the home, spin in the wind as it drew water from the lake. The oddity was destroyed in a windstorm and was never replaced. She focused on Preston standing at the wheel. He'd removed his jacket and rolled the sleeves of his white shirt up to reveal muscled forearms. Without a hat, the breeze played with his thick dark brown hair. He needed a haircut but she loved the way his locks hung over his collar. He had to be one of the most handsome men around.

As if sensing her stare, he turned to look at her over his shoulder and grinned, causing the dimple in his chin to deepen. "I'm glad I ran into you. There's something I want to discuss. Maybe tomorrow?"

"Why not today?"

"I'm not ready yet." He turned back to steer the boat and they traveled in companionable silence, as old friends often did, until Preston drew the *Ida* up to the Safe Refuge's dock and quickly got the boat anchored to a piling. He placed his hat back on his head then transferred the remains of her bicycle onto the pier. "You're next."

Maureen limped as she walked to the edge of the boat deck and took his hand as she stepped off the boat. Once both feet were securely on the pier, she grinned. "I'm glad that went smoother than my embarking."

He laughed. "Me too or I may have ended up in the water. Although I rather enjoyed your using me as a landing spot. He winked and lifted his bowler to wipe his brow. "Even though a dip in the lake would be most welcome about now."

She glanced toward the Queen Anne home her granddaddy had built after the great fire. "Ah, looks like Da spotted us. Here he comes." She raised her hand and waved.

Da, wearing dungarees held up by suspenders and a knit work shirt, that belied his current status of lakeshore property owner, returned her wave and continued walking across the grass.

As hard as she'd tried, she couldn't convince her father he could afford not to labor so hard at his florist and landscaping business and pay people to do the work. He was as much a nonconformist in his own way as she was in hers. No matter marrying into a family bred on British principles, he remained the Irish immigrant he was when he fell in love with Anna Hartwell. He reached the pier and approached them, his boot heels clip-clopping on the wood planks. A deep frown marred his face as his gaze slid from Preston to Maureen and then to the broken bicycle. "What's going on?"

She forced a smile. "Just a little mishap. Preston happened to be nearby and came to my rescue."

"From the looks of that bicycle and you, it was more than a little mishap. I knew trouble waited when you decided to ride that thing to work instead of letting me take you into town."

She raised her chin. "I've been riding it for a whole month without a bit of trouble. If I hadn't been doing something foolish it wouldn't have happened."

His left brow rose. "I'm almost afraid to ask what that foolish thing might be."

She shrugged "Pres says the bike's frame is bent, but it can be easily repaired and the front wheel reattached."

Da picked up the bicycle frame and examined it. "Doesn't look like that easy of a job."

"I think I know what to do," Preston said. "I'll take it home and work on it." Without waiting for agreement, he returned the bicycle parts to the boat.

Da's arm went around her waist. "Do you think you can walk to the house or should I carry you?"

"I can handle the walk." She glanced over her shoulder. "Preston would you like to come in for a while?"

He looked as if he was going to accept her invitation then shook his head. "I need to get back to Shelter Bay. I'll be in touch sometime tomorrow for that discussion."

"Okay." She wrapped her arm around her father's waist. "Shall we go, Da? I'm not as fast moving, so it may take me a while to get up the hill."

"Nonsense." Da swooped her up into his arms and began walking across the pier toward the shore. "Thanks for bringing her home, Preston. Say hello to your parents for me."

They arrived at the veranda and, barely winded, he set her down. She loved how strong her father was even at the old age of forty-seven. Hauling and lifting large trees in his landscaping business kept him from being weak and soft like so many men who lived on the shore and for that she was grateful.

"Your mother is off with Katie working on wedding plans. I

suggest you get yourself cleaned up before she comes home. If you don't, she probably will insist you stop going on wheel to work, and I know you don't want that to happen."

She pressed her palm against his cheek. "Thanks for the warning. I love you, Da."

MAUREEN LIMPED into the kitchen and Mama turned from where she stood pouring hot water into a tea cup. "Well, you look a lot better than how your father described your appearance after Preston brought you home. I was about to enjoy a cup of tea. Dinner won't be for another hour. Marta fixed a meatloaf for us before she went home."

Maureen sniffed the air and her stomach growled. Although Mama came to her marriage with little cooking experience, she learned and turned out a number of good meals, but there was nothing like the meatloaf their housekeeper made. She pushed out a smile. "Tea sounds wonderful and so does dinner. As for me, a bath and a change of clothes did wonders. Good thing mutton sleeves were in style to conceal the dressing she had to place over the wound on her arm.

Mama added a tea bag to a second cup then poured steaming water over it and carried both beverages to the round oak table. She set the cups down and sat. "So, what happened?"

Maureen shrugged and took her seat. "Just a little mishap. My bicycle wheel got caught in a wagon rut and before I could catch myself, I was face down in the middle of Broad Street. All I got was a mouthful of dirt and a torn shirtwaist."

Mama grimaced. "I hope you don't catch something. That dirt is not sanitary."

Maureen rolled her eyes. "I'm well aware of what is in that dirt. Did Da tell you that Preston was nearby when it happened and brought me home on the *Ida*?"

"Yes. But let's not change the subject. I hope this mishap, as you call it, has cured you of wheeling about and wearing those bloomers." She settled her green-eyed gaze over Maureen. "You're a beautiful girl and you should always be wearing something like what you have on now."

"From what you and Da have told me, it sounds like if there'd been bicycles around in your day, you'd be wearing bloomers and riding a bike to your teaching job instead of depending on someone to drive you in a buggy."

The half-smile on Mama's face faded. "If I'd done that I'd have probably been disowned by your grandmother."

Maureen laughed. "Not the grandmother I remember."

"No. Thankfully, she'd changed a lot by the time you were born. Your father said Preston is going to try to fix the bicycle."

She grinned. "He can and he will. He's very good with his hands. But not the same for brain work much to his father's disappointment."

"You do know why he is home and no longer at Yale?"

"Of course, I do."

Her mother let out a sigh. "I know you two have been close since you were little, and Preston may be the son of one of my dearest friends, but that man has never shown any signs of maturity. That prank he pulled at Yale—"

"It was only a silly fraternity thing. You've lost your sense of humor, Mama."

"I doubt I'd have ever found humor in putting someone in a coffin without any clothes on and leaving him on the main commons for the college president to find the next morning."

"He was only stripped to his underwear. Frats do those kind of initiation pranks all the time."

"It doesn't make it okay, and it wasn't for a fraternity. Didn't he and some other boy start some kind of secret society?"

"Yes, but he's not at Yale anymore. I'm sure he'll find his direction soon."

"The look I see on your face whenever you talk about him makes me nervous." She placed her hand on top of Maureen's. "I know you two have a connection, but I don't want to see you hurt or waste away your life waiting on him to grow up. I saw you sitting with Nathan Murphy, the new doctor, in church Sunday. He's a nice young man and I'm sure, eager to make some friends."

"I wasn't sitting with Nate. We only happened to be in the same pew. Granted he is easy on the eyes, as they say these days, but he's too settled for me. Marriage isn't the only option for a woman nowadays. I'm sure Nate will make some friends over time. Maybe even meet a nice woman and get married. But it won't be me."

Mama's brows rose. "You already know him as Nate?"

She shrugged. "That's what the girls are calling him. He has been noticed by the few single women my age who are still around and not already involved with someone." She didn't dare mention that she'd waited on him at the store the one and only time she sold a piece of furniture. It was a business transaction only discussing the bedroom dresser he purchased and he never asked her name.

Mama drained her cup and set it on its saucer. "I've heard something that might strike your interest. A number of titled British men who've inherited those beautiful estates in the English countryside are coming to America to court young women."

Maureen wrinkled her nose. "Young *wealthy* American woman. Women from families far wealthier than us."

I've heard the Leiter daughters ..." Mama looked off, then back at Maureen. "I know it sounds ludicrous, but my father was able to recoup most of his fortune before he passed away and left a trust for you. As you say, it's rather modest in comparison to some families, but—"

Maureen's mouth fell open. "Mother! I'm surprised you'd

even suggest such a thing after how you were nearly forced into an arranged marriage to a horrible man."

Mama gave a dismissive wave. "This is different. Nothing is arranged. There are ways to travel to Great Britain and enter the social scene there, or for the men who are interested in making a match to come to America and do the same. The decision to marry is totally up to the couple. There's no reason why if you are to fall in love, you couldn't fall in love with an English Lord. I wish we'd taken you to England to visit our family there. You are half British you know."

"And half Irish. Last I heard they don't exactly get along. I prefer to think of myself as American. I was born in America and that's what I am. The last I'd want is to live in some stuffy building that's hundreds of years old. And you seem to forget that I already have fallen in love. I don't know why you can't accept that Preston and I are meant to be together. He just doesn't know it yet."

"You only think you are in love." Mama threw up her hands and stood. "Dinner is in an hour."

CHAPTER TWO

The next day at work, the back door opened and Maureen held her breath, hoping they weren't bringing in another dear departed soul.

"Maureen?"

Her pulse ramped up and she turned. "Oh. Preston."

He stepped closer and grinned. "You act as if you were expecting someone else and I've disappointed you." He removed his hat and held it in both hands. "I'm sorry to bother you at work. I was sure after yesterday's fall you'd be home today."

"Mama tried to make me stay home, but I insisted I come." She stood and took a step toward him. "See? I am able to walk pretty well. Da brought me to work."

He nodded. "Good to see. Have you had lunch? We need to have that talk today."

She'd never seen him so serious. "I was going to work straight through so I could leave early when Da makes a delivery at three."

His face fell. "All right. Maybe later after you get home."

"I could take a short break, I suppose. As long as we don't go too far."

His face brightened. "How about a walk to Willow Park. It's close by."

She nodded. "I'll let Mr. Owen know."

She stepped into the showroom and found her boss dusting off one of the display coffins. She winced. Better finding him here and not in the embalming room. "Mr. Owen, a friend just stopped by and I'm taking a fifteen-minute break for a walk."

He frowned. "With that Stevens boy?"

"Yes. How did you know?"

"Saw him talking with ya. Be careful."

"I always am, but Preston is hardly—"

"I presume you know why he was kicked out of Yale. Just be careful. Don't want to see you get hurt."

Sometimes a girl can have too many people caring for her welfare. Unable to come up with appropriate words, she decided silence was better and she turned away. "I appreciate your concern. Thank you." The man had barely spoken two words to her the whole year she'd been working there. Of all people, the prank Pres had pulled shouldn't have disturbed Mr. Owen. He worked with the dead and sold coffins for his job. She managed a smile and approached Preston. "Let's go. You came at a perfect time. I need some fresh air."

They walked in silence down Broad Street toward Willow Park that was nicknamed Flatiron Park because of its wedge-shape. They passed the Whiting Hotel and a small lagoon without a word. When they reached the park, Maureen looked up at him. "For someone who wanted to talk you're certainly quiet."

He drew in a long breath and let it out. "I know." He gestured toward a bench. "Let's sit. I can talk better sitting and looking you in the eyes."

They settled on the bench and she faced him. He stared straight ahead in silence.

"Preston, my break is almost up. If you don't start talking soon it'll be too late."

He turned, his face serious. "Dad gave me an ultimatum. Come work for him in Chicago pushing a pencil in a stuffy office or join the military. I'm not cut out for an office job, Mo. But I'm not cut out for the military either. All that marching to orders isn't for me. I'm heading into the city tomorrow to sign up with the U.S. Life Saving Service."

She frowned. "I've never heard of that service. Is it considered military?"

"It's part of the Coast Guard. They are stationed at points on the Great Lakes and on the East coast. They serve the schooners and other craft and make rescues when the vessels are in trouble. You know how I love the water and boats."

His eyes twinkled. "For the first time in a long while I'm excited about something. I think God gave me a desire to be a helper and fixer and this fits right into my interests. When I was there yesterday at the right time to help you, I knew for certain helping is the type of thing I'm cut out to do. I worked on your bicycle last night and it's good as new. I left it at your house when I stopped there looking for you."

A knot that felt as big as a lump of coal filled Maureen's throat. She blinked at the moisture in her eyes, willing it not to spill over. How ironic he saw yesterday as a sign he was meant to go away while she saw it as a sign they were meant for each other and should take their friendship to a new level. She managed a smile she hoped looked sincere. "Oh, Pres, that sounds perfect for you. You will have leave once in a while to come back here for a few days, won't you?"

He shrugged. "I presume so. I'll write when I get settled and tell you where I'm stationed and when I do get a break, I'll let you know. I don't want to lose touch."

He slipped his arm around her waist and tugged her closer. "I'm gonna miss you, Mo."

Here they were saying goodbye, and she wanted more than anything to give him a sendoff that would hopefully wake him up to what was waiting at home. But they were out in the open. Kiss him and the news would be all over town before she arrived back at her desk.

She leaned back and looked him in the eyes. "I'll miss you too, Pres. I'm actually thinking about moving to the city soon. This town is feeling a bit stifling these days. If I do, I'll be sure to send you my new address." She pushed to her feet. "I really do need to get back to work."

He stood and offered his elbow, which she took. When they came to the hotel, she stopped and looked up at him. "Here's where we should say goodbye. It's best if I go the rest of the way alone."

He searched her face with his eyes then leaned down and kissed her on the cheek. "Maureen Quinn, you are the best thing that ever happened to me. I just hope that someday will be the right day to court you in the way you deserve."

Stunned, she pressed her finger tips to her mouth and kissed them then placed them against his lips. "I'll be waiting."

CHAPTER THREE

*P*reston Stevens leaned his elbows on the railing of the lookout and stared out at Lake Michigan's gray water, almost a perfect match to the steel gray clouds overhead. Out on the water a two-mast vessel, its sails unfurled, skimmed along the water, likely heading to Chicago. If only he could hitch a ride. He never dreamed homesickness could be this bad.

And he hadn't thought about Maureen as much as he had since he arrived at Manitou Island, Michigan a month ago. Most of the time he recalled the fun times they'd had growing up when their families would get together for picnics at each other's lakeshore homes. When the two of them were together, their parents had to work extra hard to keep an eye on them. It was a wonder they didn't do anything worse than putting ants down her little brother's pants or spying on his older brothers when they were trying to get some alone time with their sweethearts.

What he kept returning to was a more recent memory when they parted after he told her he was leaving for the USLSS and she kissed her fingers and then pressed them onto his mouth. It couldn't have been more emotional than if she'd actually kissed him. They had never kissed before, but he was certain whenever he saw her again he'd make sure they did for real.

He'd thought signing up as a surfman with the USLSS would give him the excitement he craved while doing what he loved most—being around boats and water—while helping people in distress. So far, the assignment had not provided much excitement except for a large schooner getting caught on a sand bar and, last week, when they had to rescue a woman who'd taken a dip where swimming wasn't allowed, and the skirt of her swimming costume got caught in some seaweed.

He should have taken the assignment in Massachusetts where he'd have been based on a stretch of Atlantic shoreline. But he wanted to be no farther away from home than possible and requested the North Manitou station near Traverse City, thinking being on an island in Lake Michigan would catch more excitement that being on the mainland.

His thoughts drifted to Maureen's beautiful face, her porcelain skin and her green eyes. He'd been told that she was the spitting image of her mother at that same age. No wonder Rory Quinn fell in love with her. An Irish immigrant marrying a wealthy Chicago socialite was unheard of back then, or even today. He could only hope that at the end of his two-year stint with the service, Maureen would be waiting as promised.

Blackness tinged the horizon off to the north as a wind gust slammed into him. He stumbled backwards. Arms flailing, he grabbed the lookout's railing and gripped it until the gust died down. He'd heard one of the stations on Lake Superior had wired that they'd just gone through a terrible storm and they'd had to deal with several capsized boats, thankfully with no casualties. He hadn't given it much thought as those kinds of warnings had come through before, only for the storm to dissipate before it reached them.

Off to his right, white caps licked at the craggy shoreline, the waves to at least a couple of feet. He brought his binoculars to his eyes and searched for signs of a vessel he'd seen earlier, hoping they were farther south by now. A pair of sails bobbed up above a swell then disappeared. A second later, the hull shot up, it's flag at half-mast. The distress signal! The hull had dropped out of sight again. What was the first thing he needed to do? Alert! Sound an alert. He forced his feet to move and bolted for the ladder. The storm wasn't even over them yet. Something else must be wrong with the vessel.

Heart pounding, Preston reached the ground in record time then jumped over the rails leading to the boathouse, and darted through the door of the main building that housed sleeping quarters and an office. "Alert!" he yelled. "Storm incoming and there's a two-mast in distress. The waves are rolling up two to three feet!"

At once, eight men exploded into the room from several directions, along with the coxswain, and within minutes they were at the boathouse, four men on either side of the long surf-boat. On the coxswain's call, they pushed the boat down the rails and into the choppy water. Even at the shoreline the waves were topping at several feet by then, but thanks to their training and practice they were able to climb into the boat, each at their designated positions, hands gripping the long oars that projected out on either side of the boat. The coxswain, standing at the helm, his legs slightly bent to keep his balance, hand on the steering oar, called out the cadence.

At his middle position, Preston's arms and shoulder muscles strained as the boat rocked back and forth. The wind, like an invisible wall that stood between them and the schooner, pushed back at them. Were they ever going to reach the vessel?

Preston chanced a glance at the schooner. A lone man stood on the deck, hanging onto the front mast. Ahead of Preston just in front of the coxswain, Hobart, a muscular farmer from a small town across from North Manitou Island, was struggling to get the rocket launch set that would catapult a thick rope to the ship, anchoring it to the rescue team's boat. The surf boat lurched ahead with a jolt, bringing them within firing range of the destressed vessel.

Preston's arms ached. Even with lifting weights every day to stay strong, his strength was waning. Hobart aimed and fired, and the rope landed on the deck. The man on the schooner let go of the mast and grabbed the end of the rope and, after a few tries, was able to secure it to the front mast. The ship's crew appeared on the boat's deck, ready to be transferred to the lifeboat. They were dealing with seasoned sailors.

By now, waves were washing over the surf boat's sides and several of the rowers turned to bailing as one man after the other worked his way down the rope and onto the lifeboat. The last one, the captain, a barrel-chested man, climbed into the boat and the coxswain shouted against the wind. "Is that the last of ya?"

"Yes sir. All present and accounted for."

One of the rescuers pointed at the schooner. "There's two more!"

A woman wearing a long skirt and jacket held the hand of a boy who couldn't be more than four years old while clinging to the rope with her other hand.

The captain's mouth fell open. "Where did they come from? We should have taken them first."

"A short scrawny man from the schooner climbed over several men in front of him. He cursed and yelled, "That's my wife and boy. I had no idea they were onboard. I said goodbye to them three ports back when I was hired on."

The captain's jaw pulsed. "They're stowaways. Got to get them off of there."

The coxswain shook his head. "All right men, we've got to

get those two. The lady is going to have to hold the boy as she comes down the rope."

"She'll never make it." The husband's eyes were wide with fear. "Please don't make her carry him. She just lost our daughter in childbirth and she's not strong."

Preston whispered, "Lord help me." He rose from his position. "I'll go up the rope and bring the boy down."

The coxswain looked his direction. "Okay. Stevens, get over here and get up that rope we don't have much more time."

Oh, how he wished for a breaches buoy lifeline right then, but they'd lost the one they had during a rescue a few weeks ago and the new one hadn't arrived yet. He'd have to rely on his muscles and God's strength to get to the boat, prepare the lady for transfer alone on the rope and then bring the boy with him after she was in the surfboat. He found a length of rope and attached it to his belt and held onto the connecting rope as the men pulled and got him to the ship.

He stared into the frightened face of a woman who appeared to be hardly more than a young girl. "What's your name and your son's?"

"Sally. His name is Johnny."

"Okay, Sally, you'll grab hold of the rope tight with both hands and the crew down there will start pulling, and you'll be carried over the water to the boat. Your husband is safe and waiting for you."

She pulled her son close to her side. "I'm not leaving him behind."

"I'll be bringing Johnny over. Just pray for me, okay?"

She nodded and bent to hug Johnny. "You be mama's brave boy and listen to Mr. ... She looked up at Preston.

"Preston Stevens."

"Mr. Stevens."

The boy nodded and bit on his trembling lip.

A moment later, he had Sally making the transfer and once

she was safely on the boat, he took the rope he'd brought and tied it securely around the boy's waist, then around his own waist. "Johnny, I want you to clasp your hands around my neck as tight as you can and whatever you do don't let go. Before we start off, you'll wrap your legs around my middle and keep them there. Okay?"

The boy took a deep breath and nodded. Preston got him as securely attached to himself as he could. "Lord be with me." He gripped the rope. "Johnny, remember to hang on tight."

The weight of the boy was more than he expected, and he kept talking to the lad as they began the traverse. They only had a few more feet and they'd be in the boat. A sudden wave rose up out of the water and seemed to grab onto Johnny's feet. The boy screamed and Pres held him closer to his chest. "Keep hanging on, Johnny. Don't let go."

"I can't hold anymore! I try to swim." Johnny unlocked his hands and leaned back, his head touching the water. If Preston kept hold of the rope he'd lose the boy. "Johnny straighten up."

"I can't."

The woman's screams above the roar of the wind filled his ears. The boy was slipping away. Pres let go of the rope and he and the boy hit the cold water together. Like a slippery fish, the boy slid out of the rope and Preston took a dive. He opened his eyes but saw nothing. He came to the surface and gulped in air then dove again.

His arms suddenly feeling strengthened, he reached out, felt something, and grabbed at is. He rose to the surface, relieved to see Johnny in his grasp. Remembering the lifesaving hold he learned in training, he pushed through the waves toward the boat. They were rowing toward him, but his arms felt like cement and it seemed as if they were standing still. Suddenly the surfboat was beside him, and he and the boy were dragged into the boat.

He looked over at Johnny who lay lifeless on the boat's floor. "Is he?"

"He's still alive, but barely."

They were able to ride a wave almost to the shore, and the other men jumped out and dragged the boat up onto the beach, then laid Johnny out on the sand and began artificial respiration. Preston folded into a sitting position on the sand and buried his face in his hands. "Please God let him live. If he doesn't live how can I go through life myself?"

A hand rested on his shoulder and he looked up into the coxswain's grizzled face.

"He's gone."

He cursed and scooped up a rock from the sand and threw it hard toward the lake. "I got him to the boat. He can't be gone." He scrambled to his feet and ran over and knelt in front of the child's still body. He pressed on his back, then lifted his arms, and pressed on the small back again."

"Don't you touch my son. You've done enough damage." A hand gripped Preston's arm and yanked him from the child and tossed him onto the beach as though he were a fistful of seaweed. Preston stared in the boy's father's face. The man's nostrils flared as he raised his fist. Two others, one from the ship and one from the service, grabbed the distraught man and pulled him away from Preston. "Stevens head for the house. Get out of here now!"

He needed no further instruction and did as he was commanded. Inside the house, he dropped onto a small sofa and covered his face with his hands.

He was still weeping when the outside door opened. "You have nothing to be sorry about, son. You did the brave and right thing."

He raised his head and looked at the coxswain. "But the boy died."

"I know. When something like this happens, and sometimes

it does, I've leaned on a verse from the Psalms that says God knows every day of our lives before one of them has happened. They'll be transporting the parents and the boy's remains over to the mainland in a few minutes. I suggest you remain here until they are gone. You've had enough excitement for today. You're excused from getting the boat back into the boathouse. Go clean up and get some rest."

CHAPTER FOUR

One Month Later

Despite the lingering morning chill, the sun felt warm on Maureen's face as she walked the shore path to Snug Harbor, the George Sturges estate two doors down from her family's property. The four-story home reminded her of a castle as its magnificent turret came into view.

Other than when she'd attended the estate's housewarming as a child, she'd never been beyond the veranda that stretched across the front of the home. She walked over the wide lawn, then climbed the steps and entered the large screened porch. A gathering of women sat at the far end of the veranda. Mary Sturges stood from one of the chairs. "Maureen, welcome."

Mary came forward, her long dark skirt swishing around her ankles. Her dark hair pulled back into a bun and her face as smooth as a young girl's, one would never know the widow had birthed and raised nine children and for years, had been involved in philanthropic causes. Now here she was hosting an exploratory meeting regarding women's suffrage.

Maureen accepted Mary's hand. "I must have misunderstood the time, Mrs. Sturges. I'm sorry for being late."

Mary offered a warm smile. "You're not at all late. The ladies love sitting on our veranda so much they often show up early to sit and catch up on each other's lives. And please call me Mary." She took hold of Maureen's elbow and walked her to the group. "Ladies, this is Maureen Quinn from the Safe Refuge estate.

A chorus of "hellos" and "welcomes" filled the space and Maureen nodded as she returned their smiles. They all appeared to be Mama's age. *She should be here, not me.* "Thank you for inviting me."

"We were hoping more of the younger women in town would have joined us. I'm afraid our wrinkles may have frightened them away," A blond woman said.

Maureen waved a hand. "Many of my friends are interested in the suffrage movement, but most are away at college."

One of the women stood and pulled an empty chair over next to her. "Alice Barber. I live in town, not on the lakeshore. There are plenty more of us too."

Grateful, for Alice's gesture, Maureen sat as a maid who looked to be about Maureen's age, stepped onto the porch carrying a tray of small cakes.

"The date and nut brownies have arrived." Mary said. "Ladies, before we begin our discussion, let's indulge ourselves. I had these at my brother-in-law's home up on the hill and coerced the recipe out of his cook." She faced the maid. "Ginny, can you please bring us another pot of hot water for our tea?"

"Yes, ma'am." The girl's familiar Irish accent put Maureen at ease, but also motivated her to get more involved in the suffrage movement. Her da had risen above his status through marrying Mama, but he still had to earn the respect of some of the lakeshore people. And he wasn't the only one. Being the youngest one here, she had to do the same. She took a brownie and napkin from the plate Mary held out and quietly listened to the conversation.

"You say your friends have all returned to college. Is there a reason you decided to not follow the crowd—if you are willing to share?"

Snapped out of her reverie, Maureen faced Alice and realized she was near her own age. "I'm unsettled in my plans and am taking time to figure it all out."

"I'm sorry for my boldness," Alice said. "My husband, Joel, always tells me to think twice before I speak." She picked up her cup and sipped. "Too much time spent in academia, I guess."

Maureen stared at her. Perhaps she misread the woman's age. "Academia. Do you mean college?"

She nodded. "I went to dental school after graduating from university. I'm a dentist."

"Where? In Chicago?"

The woman's eyes twinkled as a broad smile filled her features. "Oh, no. Too large for me. Right here in Lake Geneva."

Maureen gaped, "I had no idea. Are you there every day?"

"Currently, I'm keeping half days. I had a baby girl several months ago. When she gets a little older I'll go back to full hours. I'm open Monday through Friday and Saturday mornings from nine until noon.

Maureen took a bite of the brownie and something crunched in her mouth. Much too loud for a small nut. She chewed a tiny bit and her teeth hit something hard. She deposited whatever it was in the napkin then peeked into the cloth and gasped. "I think I just broke a tooth." She ran her tongue over her teeth until it touched a ragged tooth in the back.

"Let me see." Alice bent toward Maureen and peered into the napkin. "A molar broke off. It looks to be a wisdom tooth. It's best to pull it. I'm open this afternoon since I came to this meeting this morning. If you can come to my office this afternoon at two-thirty I can look at it then. I'm on the first floor in the Metropolitan Building."

Maureen blinked. "The one at Main and Broad? I've never noticed a dentist office in there."

Alice's eyes twinkled "I'm tucked in the back. My professional name is Doctor Sherman, my maiden name. I started the practice before I married, and I didn't think Dr. Barber would go over too well, since barbers have been pulling teeth for years." She frowned. "Are you in pain?"

She shook her head. Visions of Alice using a pair of pliers to pull out the rest of her tooth swirled in her thoughts. She'd heard horror stories from people who'd had their teeth pulled by a barber. One ended up with an infection that took months to clear up. Maybe she could live with the broken tooth as long as she was careful to chew on the opposite side. She ran her tongue over the ragged tooth. She couldn't live with that the rest of her life. Alice was a trained dentist, not a barber. "I'll be there at two thirty."

Mary called the meeting to order. After an hour and a half of rousing discussion about next steps to move toward spreading the word about the movement in their area and rights for women in general, the meeting ended. It was decided the next meeting would be in October at Alice Barber's home on Dodge Street.

Maureen had made the right decision not going into work today. Not only was it fortuitous that she met Alice at the very moment she needed a dentist, but she hoped to learn some tips into forging into occupations generally considered for men only. There was no reason why she could not do the same to accomplish her dream

LATER THAT AFTERNOON, Maureen took the side entrance into the Metropolitan Building and turned right at the hallway that ran the length of the structure. No wonder she hadn't seen Alice's dental office. She'd never come this far down the hall.

She reached the last door on the right and opened it. A plump gray-haired woman looked up from her writing. "Good afternoon, may I help you?"

Maureen stepped inside the tiny waiting area. "Yes. I have a two-thirty appointment with Al ... Dr. Sherman."

The woman stood. "You must be Maureen Quinn. Dr. Sherman is waiting for you. All I need is your mailing address on this card and then you can go in." Maureen scribbled the requested information on the card, then followed the woman to a door on her left. Maureen stepped past her and entered the room.

Careful not to look at the unusual chair sitting front and center, she focused on Alice who stood at the window overlooking Broad Street wearing a long white jacket similar to what she'd seen Dr. Kiley, the family's doctor wear.

Alice turned. "Maureen, I'm so glad you didn't change your mind. Go ahead and sit in the chair. I was trying to get this window up a bit higher. It's so warm in here." She looked past Maureen. "Dora, can you help me with this window before you wash up?"

Dora scurried over. "Of course, Doctor."

Alice stepped over to a small sink and began washing her hands. "Take a minute to look at everything if you like, Maureen. I usually get the same stunned reaction from people who've never been to a dental office."

Grateful for time to gather herself, Maureen scanned the room, taking in a wood cabinet that contained at least a dozen small flat drawers and next to that, a tall bookcase filled with what appeared to be text books, all important and protected behind glass doors. But most of her focus was on the seat of torture, otherwise known as the chair.

Alice dried her hands on a small towel that hung next to the sink. "Intimidating isn't it?"

Maureen nodded.

"Why don't you sit in the chair and let me determine how to get the tooth out as painlessly as possible."

Maureen sat on the edge of the hard seat while Alice adjusted the head rest then asked her to lean back.

Dora managed to prop the window open by inserting a stick then went to the washbowl. While water ran in the background, Alice donned a face mask then leaned over Maureen and asked her to open her mouth. She picked up an ivory-handled mirror. "I'm going to use this little tool to get a closer look. It will feel odd to have something like this in your mouth. She inserted the mirror.

The doctor's eyes widened then the lines above her nose deepened and her eyes narrowed. She removed the mirror and leaned back, pulling the face mask down at the same time. "A good-sized chunk of tooth broke off, as we already knew. I think I can pull it without it breaking it in two. Dora, prepare a teaspoon of laudanum"

Maureen scrunched her face and turned her head. "No. The last time I took laudanum, it knocked me out cold for two days."

Alice frowned. "I don't think you'll need that strong a dose. If I don't use it, this will hurt a lot."

"I can handle it."

"I could give you laughing gas. But there are side effects with that as well."

Maureen shook her head. "No thanks."

"You impress me. Even the biggest men quake at the thought of getting a shot or having a tooth pulled without a painkiller."

"Doesn't mean I'm being brave. I just don't like the way those drugs make me lose control of things. I don't even like drinking alcohol for that reason. Let's get it done." She sat back and opened her mouth.

Alice picked up what looked like a pair of pliers with very long handles. "I'm going to work the tooth back and forth a bit with these forceps, then grip it tight and pull it out. You'll feel a lot of pressure along with the pain. I'll try to get it out as fast as possible. Here we go."

She poked the business end of the forceps into Maureen's mouth and moved it around. A clicking sound came." "Okay. I've got a good grip on the tooth. The pressure is going to start now."

Alice pushed against the tooth and pressure against Maureen's jaw mounted. The dentist pushed the opposite direction, and it felt as if the tooth was going the snap off at the root. She switched direction again. So far, the pain wasn't too bad. "I'm going to start pulling now, Maureen. It's going to hurt but stay as still as you can."

Maureen squeezed her eyes shut as sharp pain shot down her neck and into her spine. She gripped the chair handles until she thought she'd break them in two. Tears trailed down her cheeks and Dora dabbed at them with a soft cloth. She forced her thoughts onto Preston's handsome face and how it would feel to be in his arms. Maybe she could take a train to where he was in Michigan. She'd walk up the beach and see him keeping watch in the lookout station he described in his last letter. He'd look down. Then grinning like a jack-o-lantern, he'd scramble down the ladder and run to her, scoop her up in his arms, and whirl her around. Then he'd set her down and bring his lips to hers and—.

"It's out and all in one piece."

Maureen's eyes popped open and Alice held up several pieces of gauze folded into a square. "I'm going to press these onto the wound. Don't move." Suddenly her fingers were back in Maureen's mouth. "Close your mouth gently. Whatever you do, don't talk for at least an hour. Dora will give you more gauze. After a couple of hours, you can change the dressing. Don't do any sucking. It will break the clot. When you eat later tonight, eat only soft foods like a soft-boiled egg or mashed potatoes. Within a week you'll be nearly healed. In the meantime, chew on the opposite side of your mouth. Now sit still for a minute and gather your strength." She held up the forceps with what was left of Maureen's tooth still in its grip. A long bloody root extended below the pinchers. Maureen turned away and her stomach heaved.

Alice laid the forceps on a tray. "I'm sorry. Since you were so brave I assumed you'd want to see what I removed."

Maureen shook her head.

A few minutes later, Alice helped Maureen out of the chair and walked her into the waiting room. She held up her leather purse, but Alice waved it away. "No charge. She handed her a small envelope of laudanum and more gauze in another envelope. "These kinds of wounds seem to hurt worse when one is quiet and trying to sleep. You may want to take a half teaspoon of the laudanum tonight before you go to bed. It will help you sleep and you shouldn't have any of the bad effects you had before." Maureen released her purse's clasp and Alice slipped the envelope containing the pain killer inside and then the gauze.

"Remember the next meeting for our group is a month from now at my house. I'll send a note out to remind you, unless you have a telephone. We had ours installed last week."

Maureen shook her head.

"No problem. I'll send a note."

Right about then Maureen wished they had a telephone. If they did, she'd call for Da to come and get her.

A half hour later, her mouth throbbing, Maureen stepped through her home's side door, hoping to sneak up the back stairs to the second floor and go straight to her room. She stepped into the kitchen and came to a halt. Across the room, Mama, Da, and her teen-age brother Richard stood huddled around Mr. Wardingle who worked for the new telephone company. He'd been trying to convince Da to install a telephone at the house. But Da hadn't yet been convinced it wasn't more than a passing novelty. He'd gotten along fine using letters and word of mouth. Had Mr. Wardingle worn down Da after all? Or Mama who'd said more than once it would be nice to be able to talk to her sister, Callie, who had a phone installed at her Chicago area home several months ago.

"Now all you have to do is wind this little crank right here." Mr. Wardingle turned a handle on the side of a wooden box affixed to the wall. "Then pick up the earpiece and hold it to your ear and wait for the operator to answer." He lifted a tubular-shaped thing that hung on the other side of the box and pressed it to his ear.

He spoke into what looked like a tiny megaphone extending from the box. His raised voice filled the room. "Hello, Mabel. It's Frank. I'm hooking up the Quinn's new telephone. Can you put me through to my home?" He turned and looked over at the others. "I hope my wife is home. There she is." He turned back to the mouthpiece. "Hi, Edith." His raised voice was back. "I'm calling from the Quinn home. Do you have a minute to speak to them so they can hear how well this works?" He nodded and handed the earpiece to Da and tugged him by the elbow closer to the telephone. "Be sure to speak here." He pointed at the tiny megaphone.

"Hello, Edith. This is Rory Quinn." A smile broke out on his face. "Yes, I hear you fine. Here's Anna." He handed Mama the earpiece, then glanced at Maureen. A deep V formed between his brows. "Good heavens, Mo, what happened to your face?"

Maureen placed her palm over her cheek. It felt twice as large as it had when she left Alice's office. She must look like a squirrel storing up nuts for the winter. She pointed to her face then mimed the motion of pulling something from her mouth.

Mama handed the earpiece to Mr. Wardingle and stepped closer to Maureen. "I can't understand you. You look like you were in a fist fight."

She shook her head and opened her mouth and pointed into it. Mama grimaced and turned her head away. Maureen clamped her mouth shut.

"Why didn't you tell me you had a bad tooth? I hope you didn't go to that barber over on Center Street. He claims he knows best how to pull a tooth, but don't tell that to Hilda Conroy."

Maureen shook her head, wishing she could talk, and pointed to the ceiling.

Her mother nodded. "Yes. Go up to your room and get in bed. I'll bring you some laudanum in a few minutes."

Maureen shook her head and held up the envelope Alice had given her.

"I know you had a bad reaction to it a couple of years ago, but a little will ease the pain. If you change your mind . . . I almost forgot. This came for you in today's mail." She pulled an envelope from her skirt pocket.

Maureen snatched up the mail and scurried for the stairs, willing herself to not look at who it was from until she was alone.

CHAPTER FIVE

$\mathcal{M}$aureen leaned against the closed bedroom door and turned the envelope over. It hurt too much to grin, but if she could breathe in the scent of Preston that would suffice. She lifted it and sniffed, but only the lingering scent of her mother's rose water tickled her nose.

She set the envelope on the nightstand next to her canopied bed, then removed her shirtwaist and skirt and tossed the garments on the upholstered chair. Not bothering to remove her camisole, she slid under the covers and picked up Preston's letter. He may not be around now to comfort her, but reading his words was the next best thing. She slid her finger under the seal and the envelope unfolded to expose a page filled with tiny writing. He must be distressed. He usually wrote no more than two paragraphs in a letter.

Dearest Mo,

I'm sorry I've not written recently. there hasn't been much to tell. Until a few days ago every day has been the same.

Last Monday, a huge storm came down from the north and something so terrible happened that I cannot bear to write about it here. I've been as if paralyzed ever since. I have been told to take three days leave. I'm hoping you can arrange to meet me in Chicago to attend the Columbian Exposition.

I plan to take the 1:00 p.m. train out of Traverse City to Chicago on August 23rd. I have to leave the afternoon of the 25th to be back here by midnight. if you take the train from Lake Geneva that arrives at 3:25 p.m. that same day, I can meet you at the Northwestern Depot. I'm hoping you'll be able to stay with your friend Sophie. If not, I'll arrange a hotel room for you.

Please telegraph me if you can do this. Also, please pray I will be able to function well until I leave for Chicago or they might discharge me. If I am booted out, I don't think my dad will ever forgive me.

With all my affection,

Preston

Maureen pressed the letter to her chest. What in the world happened? He was the most fearless man she knew. How was he paralyzed? With fear? Sadness?

A large knot filled her throat. She looked at the ceiling and let go of a sob. "Please God, give him strength to get through the days ahead."

A knock came at the door. "Maureen, are you all right?"

"Yes. Come in."

The door opened and her sister, Katie, entered the room, worry lines marring her face.

"Are you sure you're okay?"

She turned away. "Yes."

"Then what was that sob I heard?"

"I had a tooth pulled this afternoon, and it hurts a lot. It must be swollen."

"Not only swollen, but black and blue. What did that barber do to you?"

"I didn't go to a barber. Did you know Lake Geneva has a woman dentist?"

Katie's eyes widened. "Where?"

"In the Metropolitan Building. She's really nice. I met her this morning at a gathering at Snug Harbor."

Katie rolled her eyes. "Let me guess. For a discussion on women's suffrage."

"What if it was? Women can be mothers and housewives and at the same time, be smart enough to vote and do other things ascribed only to men."

Her sister dropped her gaze. "I know, but why do you have to be one of the ones to be so outspoken? It will only draw attention to our family."

"We've nothing to hide. If we can be part of the movement to give women the right to vote, we'll be seen in a positive way."

Her sister looked off toward the window. "For some, yes. I'm old enough to remember when the family name had been dirtied and how many people shunned us. It's taken a lot of years for the community to see us in a positive way. We don't need a setback."

"Oh, that was long ago. I doubt anyone even remembers what happened."

"I wouldn't count on it. Some of the older ladies at church still try to avoid us when they can. They remember."

Maureen sighed. "Remind me to ask what exactly happened back then, but not now." She held up Preston's letter. "This came today. Something awful has happened to Preston. He wouldn't talk about it in his letter, but he's getting a few days leave and wants to meet me in Chicago next week to attend the Columbian Exposition. I plan to go."

"Are you sure you want to do that? What about that serial killer who's running loose?"

"I plan to only go for a couple of nights, and I won't be going to the fair alone. Preston will be with me. I'm going to telegraph

Sophie Benson from college and see if I can stay with her. Pres will be at his family's home."

Katie's right brow lifted. "Every time he's led you to think he's ready to settle down he gets in a peck of trouble. That's the very reason he's been exiled to the wilds of northern Michigan."

Maureen frowned. How was it she seemed to be the only one who believed in Preston? "He's not exiled. Joining the rescue service was his idea."

Katie huffed a breath. "Not the story I heard."

"What did you hear?"

"That he was given an ultimatum after he was expelled from Yale—to work for his father in Chicago or get a job up here in Lake Geneva. When he chose neither, his father arranged for a stint in the U.S. Life-Saving Service."

Was nothing private in this town? "Who told you that? He signed up on his own accord."

"Take it from your sister, who has seven more years under her hat. Avoid him." She turned to leave.

"I thought you'd be happy for me."

Katie faced her, her blue-eyed gaze boring into Maureen. "I do understand. But not the way you do. By the way, we're due for a fitting at Millie's tomorrow at three. Your bridesmaid dress and Doreen's flower girl dress are both ready, and so is my gown. Can you leave work a bit early?"

"Three will be fine. Mr. Owen won't mind, but even if he does, I plan to quit that job soon anyway."

"Quit? Why?"

"How would you like to work in a place where you have to endure dead bodies being carried past your desk?"

"I wouldn't, but you knew when you took the bookkeeper position that Mr. Owen was also the town undertaker."

"Yes, but I didn't think I'd have to see the corpses carried past me every time someone dies."

"They are covered, right?"

"Most of the time. The other day, the covering lifted in the breeze as they carried the body in on a stretcher." She winced. "There was old man Fitzsimmons in all his grotesque glory. Not to mention that awful smell that drifts upstairs while they are embalming."

Katie grimaced. "Well, I advise you to find something else before quitting. Maybe you can work for Da."

"I'm thinking that maybe while I'm in the city I'll head over to the Pinkerton Agency and apply."

Katie quirked her head. "Apply for what?"

"To be an apprentice detective. You know how that's been my dream since I was little."

"I thought it was only a childhood fantasy." Her eyes widened. "Do you really think they'd hire a woman?"

"They've had women detectives for over twenty years. Since I hate my present job and Preston is going to be tied up for two years, why not give it a try?"

"Are you going to tell Mama and Da about this idea or just spring it on them if and when you are hired?"

"The latter is the best course I would think. I always thought Mama was more of a risk-taker than she seems to be now. She stood up to Granddaddy and Granny when she refused to go through with that arranged marriage."

Katie nodded. "And fell in love with Da which set Granny into a tailspin."

Maureen grinned. "I love hearing how after Da thought you had died in the fire and you showed up at a town picnic."

Katie palmed a tear that was trickling down her face. "I remember it as if it were yesterday. I thought I was an orphan and suddenly there was Uncle Rory." She giggled. "I took off running across the field and Miss Anna tripped trying to catch me. It's not every girl whose uncle is also her father and her teacher becomes her mother."

Maureen leaned over and hugged her sister. "Do you ever miss your real mother?"

Katie shrugged. "I barely remember her except for the way she smelled all nice and clean from the soap she used and when she hugged me before bedtime. Da has the same laugh as hers and the way he looks at me is the same way I remember my mother looking at me. Sometimes it feels as though she is still with me." She pinned her gaze on Maureen. "Our family's legacy is important to keep up. Please keep that in mind."

"What is our legacy? I have never figured it out."

"Rising against the odds, breaking down walls between the privileged and under privileged, honoring God with our lives. That's how I see it."

"That's a lot to live up to. I'll leave it up to you and our brother and sister to follow in those footsteps."

"I see you rising up against the odds. Getting involved in the suffrage movement is one thing."

"I haven't seen much support from our parents in that. It seems once they were able to marry, they weren't so strong in that resolve.

Katie rested a fist on her hip. "You know that's not true. Mama continued teaching at Woods School after they were married and up until a couple of months before you were born. If she had wanted to return to teaching, Da would have supported her."

"I doubt it."

"Don't forget he was working class and women often had to help bring in money one way or another. Many took in laundry or became household staff at one of the estates on the lake. Mama tutored students from home for many years."

"I'd forgotten that. Why did she stop?"

"I don't know exactly. You'd have to ask her. If you want to get more involved in the community, I heard Mrs. Sturges donated her cottage on Main Street as well as the surrounding property to the city for the express purpose of using it as a library and park. You like to read. Why don't you look into joining the women's group who is overseeing the project?"

"Mary did that? She never mentioned it at the meeting this morning, but even so, those ladies are old and married."

"They are more mature, as I like to say, but wiser for their years than us. You can learn a lot from them."

"Then why don't you join the movement?"

"Perhaps I will after the wedding and things settle. I'll still be teaching at Woods, so I won't have much time to keep our home and help my husband with the farm."

"Not the life you were raised in, is it?"

"No. But I wasn't born to this kind of life to begin with. Please promise me you will keep this conversation in mind as you make decisions. Now lie back and rest. You've been doing too much talking for someone who had a tooth pulled a few hours ago."

CHAPTER SIX

Two Weeks Later

Maureen waved at Da then turned and climbed the steps into the train car. She moved down the aisle between the brown cushioned seats, most empty, and selected one next to a window. She slid her leather suitcase in front of the seat then sat with her knees pressed up against her bag and faced the glass.

Da still sat in his wagon, his eyes moving back and forth as though looking for her. She waved as his gaze swept past her window.

He lifted his hand and blew her a kiss. Tears welled in her eyes. He was never shy about showing affection in public. Not to Mama or his children. And she loved him for that. She pressed her fingertips to her lips and blew him a kiss in return as the conductor called out, "All aboard." The train lurched then proceeded down the track, crossing Broad Street and leaving Da behind.

What she loved most about her father was his deep faith in God and how he prayed for each of his children and Mama every morning. He was no doubt praying for her now as he headed to his work. He hadn't liked the idea of her traveling into the city alone, even if Preston was meeting her at the depot. Despite his not saying anything, she knew he wasn't happy about her growing affection for Pres. And that probably is what was troubling him the most.

Mama was more vocal. Her words from earlier still echoed in her mind. "Don't say I didn't warn you, Maureen. I don't trust that young man. He has too much youthful mischievousness in him. A man of his age should be more settled and responsible."

She rested her head against the back of the seat and closed her eyes. It was wonderful to hear Preston's voice last night when he telephoned to confirm her train's arrival time and to assure he'd be there to meet her train. When she'd telegraphed him to say she would meet him as he asked, she'd mentioned their new telephone, but never expected him to call.

He sounded normal and never mentioned the trouble he talked about in his letter. Maybe by now it all had passed. His final words before they ended last night's short conversation about sent her stomach into a fluttering frenzy. "I can't wait to see you, Mo, and give you a proper hug." In about two hours she'd be in his arms.

At Genoa Junction at the Illinois-Wisconsin state line, the train rolled to a stop to take on passengers. She feigned sleep in hopes no one would sit beside her. As much as she enjoyed conversation with most anyone, today she wanted to be alone in her thoughts. Several people stepped past her and she opened her eyes. That must have been the last of them. She shut her eyes to return to her daydream.

The adjacent seat cushion expelled a loud poof of air and her eyes popped open. An elderly woman dropped into the seat, huffing and puffing as she worked at squeezing a carpetbag, that appeared old enough to be from the war between the states, beneath her seat. When only a small portion of the bag protruded, she rested her feet on it like a footstool, opened a small cloth bag, and took out her knitting.

The old woman glanced at Maureen. "Name's Mrs. Grundy. No worries about trying to carry on a conversation. I'm not much for talking and I need to finish this sweater before I get to Chicago. It's for my new grandbaby."

Maureen glanced at the yellow yarn. "My name is Maureen. I was hoping to nap so no conversation agrees with me." She carefully removed the pins from her hat and set the bowler on her lap, then shut her eyes, certain she wouldn't sleep a wink.

"Last stop. Chicago, Illinois." At the conductor's voice, Maureen yawned and faced the window. Tall buildings whizzed past and the train slowed. She patted her hair. What she needed was a mirror.

Next to her, Mrs. Grundy stuffed her knitting into its bag. "Not quite finished."

Glad she'd worn the smaller of the two hats she brought with her, Maureen set her hat on her head and made sure the flowered adornment was positioned in the right place. After securing the hat with the pins she pinched her cheeks several times to liven the color. Without a mirror that was the best grooming she could do.

The train lurched to a stop and Mrs. Grundy stood and worked the carpet bag out from beneath her seat. She moved into the aisle. "Have a nice day, Colleen."

Maureen glanced around. The woman was looking at her as if waiting for a response. She pushed out a smile "Yes, you too. Enjoy that new grandchild."

Without another word, the elderly woman shuffled toward the door.

Maureen waited until the other passengers had cleared the aisle then made her way to the exit. The conductor stood next to the bottom step. He took her suitcase, then offered his hand to assist her. Remembering her manners, she fished a coin out of her skirt pocket and handed it to him.

She walked a short distance on the cobblestone platform then stopped and scanned the milling crowd. Of course, she didn't expect Preston to come out to the train, but one could hope. The suitcase was heavy and there wasn't even a depot worker to help. She gripped her bag and marched down the platform toward the depot entrance.

By the time she walked inside, her arm ached. She set down her case. People scurried past her, heading for the door that led to departing trains. Someone jostled her arm. She stumbled to right herself and saw the backside of the offender pushing open the outside door. She turned back the direction she'd been going. A scattering of people sat on long wood benches reading newspapers or anxiously staring at the large clock on the wall.

Across the way, a tall man bent and drew her former seat-mate into a hug, swallowing her tiny form in his arms. Perhaps he was the father of the new grandbaby? He picked up the old lady's carpet bag and with his other hand gripped her elbow as he led her to the doors facing the street.

Next to Maureen, a young man shouted, "Annie!" as he rushed up to a blond woman and wrapped his arms around her. Feeling like she was watching a private moment, she turned away. Preston said he thought he could be there by the time her train arrived, but apparently, he was wrong. What if something happened and he missed his train or it was delayed and was still in Michigan?

Then she saw him scanning the crowd, turning one direction and then the other.

"Preston!"

He was walking away from her. She had to get his attention. What if he thought she wasn't on the train? She grabbed up her suitcase and scurried toward where he'd disappeared into the swarm. She spotted the top of his head. "Preston!"

He turned and his eyes lit up.

She moved her feet as fast as she could his direction, but he'd vanished into the mob of people. At least he saw her.

His hand waved above the crowd and he popped out from behind a family, sidestepping around a man's cane.

She let go of her suitcase and ran into his open arms.

He lifted her off the floor and she wrapped her arms around his waist as they spun around.

"You are a sight to behold, Mo." He set her down and she tipped her head back and stared into the same blue eyes that always gave her a tingly feeling.

He lowered his head. Lips soft and warm caressed hers. She brought her hand to his neck and kissed him back, drinking in his touch, his scent, and the roughness of his jaw. Their first kiss was better than she ever dreamed. But she needed to breathe. She pressed her palms against his chest, and he lowered her to the ground. She glanced around. People stared their direction, wearing wide grins. Her face heated and she took a step back.

He offered a sheepish grin. "Forgot myself for a minute. That wasn't the way I wanted our first kiss to happen—in the middle of a train depot."

She snickered. "I loved it. But I don't think I'll be telling Mama about it."

He laughed and picked up her suitcase. "No, I guess you shouldn't. I have a hansom cab waiting."

Outside, the sun felt good on her face as she let him lead her down the sidewalk. They approached a cab and the driver stepped down from his seat and opened the compartment door. Pres handed Maureen's suitcase to the man, then helped her inside. He gave Sophie's address to the driver and slid onto the seat next to her. "We've about a twenty-minute ride to Sophie's. Then I'm only about five minutes longer. He slid his arm across her shoulders. "Don't eat anything at Sophie's. We'll have plenty to eat at the fair. I hear they have wonderful food. Have you ever tasted—"

She pressed her hand on his arm. Pres, what's wrong"

He blinked. "Wrong? Why?"

You never talk this much. And what you wrote me in the letter has me worried. Why do you have this leave after such a short time? Something must be wrong. Does it have anything to do with the storm you mentioned?"

He looked off. "Yes. The storm was one I'll never forget. But that's all behind me now."

"Is it?"

He turned back to her, searching her face with his eyes. He leaned in and kissed her. "Here is not the place to discuss it. Later when we're alone."

"Going to the fair doesn't sound like being alone. We don't have but a couple of days."

The cab came to a stop. They were at Sophie's already. Preston leaned toward her and pressed a kiss on her forehead. I'll be back for you in about fifteen minutes. Is that enough time?"

"Yes."

"Good." He opened the compartment door and climbed out, then took Maureen's hand and helped her step down. She didn't want to let go of his hand, and by the way he gripped her, it didn't seem he wanted to either. But he did.

He looked at the driver. "I'll carry her bag to the door and be back in a minute."

They walked side by side to the limestone townhouse and as they took the four steps to the small stoop, the door swung open. Sophie stood there, her blond curls immaculately dressed into an up do and, as always, wearing the latest fashion—a pale blue shirtwaist and navy skirt that grazed her ankles.

She smiled and gathered Maureen into a hug. "Mo, I'm so glad you made it." She then shifted her gaze to Preston. "You must be Preston. Maureen has spoken of you often. I'm glad we finally meet."

He accepted her outreached hand and nodded. "Likewise. I'm sorry to run, but the driver has to deliver me to my family's home. I'll return for Mo in about fifteen minutes. We're excited to see the fair. Have you been?"

Her face lit up. "Oh yes. Several times. It's quite wonderful."

The women waited on the stoop until he climbed in the cab. Sophie faced Maureen. "He's as handsome as you described, but his eyes looked so troubled."

"I know." Maureen picked up her suitcase. "Something bad must have happened and I've only three days to find out what."

CHAPTER SEVEN

$\mathcal{M}$aureen followed Sophie through the brownstone's entryway and up the stairs that ran along the wall to their right. She'd been here once before, but it had been after a Christmas break a year ago when she stayed with Sophie until they took a train back to college. Since then, the walls had been painted a soft gray. Much better than the dreary light brown she recalled.

Sophie turned into the first room in the upstairs hall. "You're in this guestroom. I'm in the next room. She pointed to a door. "Our rooms are connected. I don't know why they are, except maybe the family had young children and it made it easier to check on them. Regardless, we can visit as long as we like tonight. Now, for the most important question of the day. What is going on with Preston and you?"

Maureen set her suitcase on the bed and flipped it open. "I wish I knew. He wrote me a very mysterious letter asking to meet him today as he had the time off. All he mentioned was a terrible storm. Something must have happened. Lake Geneva has had its share of bad storms when he's been out on the water, and he's handled them courageously. Nothing ever seems to frighten him."

She removed a dress, a pair of skirts and several shirtwaists from her bag and hung them in the armoire. She glanced down at what she had on. "A little wrinkled from the train but does this look okay for the fair? Is a suit too formal?"

Sophie waved a hand. "You will see all manner of dress there. But I think the jacket will be too warm. You'll look fine without it. That color of your blouse makes your eyes appear even greener than they are."

Maureen gathered her nightgown and undergarments from the suitcase and placed them in the top drawer of the mahogany dresser, then raised her gaze to the mirror affixed to the wall. "At least my hair survived the trip."

Sophie laughed. "You were only on the train for a couple of hours. You love him, don't you?

Her face tingled, and her reflection confirmed it was turning red as a tomato, Maureen spun around. "Does it show?"

"Well I doubt he noticed. Men are rather obtuse that way, which is a good thing. You don't want him to know too soon how you feel."

She sighed. "We've been friends since we were kids. He's been saying some things that make me think he feels the same, but then he's said similar things before in a friends-only sort of way." She touched her fingertips to her lips. "But he's never kissed me until today."

Sophie's eyes widened. "He kissed you?"

Heat filled her cheeks again but she couldn't stop her grin. "In the middle of the Northwestern Depot. Sophie, I couldn't imagine a first kiss being any better. It left my head spinning and stomach flipping. He later apologized for being so bold to carry on like that in public."

Sophie snickered. "Knowing you, you probably loved every minute."

"I did until I realized every eye in the place was focused on us."

"With disparaging looks?"

Maureen shook her head and smiled. "Hardly. They were all grinning."

"Everyone loves romance." A series of tinkling chimes sounded from downstairs. "There's the front door bell. Your chariot awaits, Cinderella."

Maureen laughed. "I wonder if he has my glass slipper."

Sophie walked to the bedroom door and waited for Maureen to pass by. "If I'm asleep when you get back, wake me. I'll want to hear every detail you're willing to share."

Maureen winked. "We'll see." She scurried down the stairs and opened the front door.

Preston removed his white straw boater and gave a slight bow. "Are you ready to take in the magnificent exposition we've heard so much about?"

Maureen giggled, pleased to see his spirits had lifted. "I certainly am." She peered around him. "No cab?"

He offered his elbow. "If we walk four blocks down we can pick up the train. We'll get off downtown because I have a surprise."

She grinned at him. "What kind of surprise?"

He offered her a heart-stopping smile. "If I told you, it wouldn't be a surprise, would it?"

"Oh, Pres, you know how I hate surprises."

He laughed. She loved how he was enjoying himself, no matter if it were at her expense. She gripped his elbow. "Except for the surprising kiss you greeted me with at the depot. That was a surprise I'll take anytime."

He smiled down at her. "I love hearing that." He pressed his palm over top of her hand that gripped his arm and his gaze went to her mouth.

Was he going to kiss her right there on the street? As much

as she wouldn't mind, she could cause embarrassment to Sophie if people knew a woman allowing such behavior in the open was a guest of the Bensons. She looked off. "I suppose I can stand the wait since you seem to be having so much pleasure out of it all."

They walked the rest of the way to the train with no more than lighthearted conversation. As much as she ached to ask about the storm that caused so much anguish, the timing wasn't right. They arrived at the train stop and climbed the steps to the platform where Pres bought two tickets. They'd only waited a few minutes when the train arrived.

They settled in two seats together and Pres took her hand and squeezed. Never had he made such romantic gestures in public. At least not everything the storm brought out of him was bad. Outside the window buildings whizzed by. Every so often, Maureen caught a flashing glimpse of Lake Michigan between the structures. The car continued to fill at stops along the way until they halted at a downtown station and Preston announced this was their stop.

They exited and as the train pulled away, Lake Michigan came into view and a cool breeze wafted over them. She turned and stared at the tall buildings a short distance away. It seemed every time she came to the city more skyscrapers had been built. Now that a dependable elevator had been invented, buildings were projected to be built as high as fifteen stories.

She turned and faced the lake, as blue as Geneva Lake but no comparison in terms of size. Like the ocean, the water appeared to extend into infinity. "Can we linger here a moment and take in the view?"

"No need, because that's the direction we're going." He gripped her arm as they crossed a street and continued toward a sign that read, WORLD'S FAIR STEAMSHIP COMPANY.

Maureen gasped. "We can take a steamship to the fairgrounds?"

His face brightened. "Do you like your surprise?"

She had to refrain from bouncing on her toes or hugging him. "Oh yes. I've always wanted to ride a steamship. I mean one larger than the ones on our lake at home."

"Tomorrow we'll take the train like most people. I thought you'd enjoy a boat ride and, since it's such a beautiful and clear day, I think the short trip will be fun. Here comes the *Christopher Columbus* now. Let's hurry and get the tickets."

Within a few minutes they'd obtained their passes and stepped through a gate onto a dock. Ahead, the steamship came toward them, its upper deck crowded with people. Maureen couldn't stop grinning. She'd never been on a boat on Lake Michigan before. And now her life-saving-rescue man was going to take her on the very lake where he served.

The vessel pulled up to the dock, and a couple of men jumped off and tied thick ropes around metal brackets affixed to the pilings along the side of the pier. They then placed a gangplank between the boat deck and the pier. Holding hands, Maureen and Preston joined a crowd of other fairgoers and waited for the steamer to empty its load of passengers. Preston's hold on her hand tightened and became clammy. She longed to pull out of his grip but didn't want to make an issue of it.

The last person finally stepped off the boat and as Maureen and Preston approached the gangplank, his grip on her hand tightened even more. They stepped onto the vessel and were directed to the upper deck. Maureen wanted in the worst way to pull her hand away from his, but he held her so tight she didn't dare try. What was wrong with him? She found an open space along the rail that would face the water during the trip and pulled him that direction.

He tugged harder and guided her across the deck to the other side. "I want to observe the city as we head down shore. We can be on the other side when we return."

This was not a battle to fight, and she allowed him to lead

her to an empty spot next to an older couple. He let go of her hand and gripped the railing with both hands until the whites of his knuckles showed. If one didn't know better they'd think the man had never been on a boat before.

Maureen peered down the dock toward the shore and pointed. "Isn't that a new building? It's quite beautiful."

He didn't answer and she glanced over. He'd bent to rest his forehead on the railing. With his eyes closed she didn't know if he was praying or resting. She placed her hand on his arm and he jumped and stood up straight.

"Pres are you ill?"

He shook his head. "I'm fine. Just tired because I didn't get much sleep last night."

The engine became louder, and on the dock below, crew members released the ropes and tossed them onto the deck. A loud horn tooted and the boat moved backward into the lake, then pointed south and picked up speed. Maureen studied Preston who was leaning his elbows on the railing again and staring at the water below. Never had she seen his face that pale or his expression so rigid. She hesitantly placed a hand on his arm, and he flicked it away, then unbuttoned his shirt's top button and loosened his tie. He was working himself out of his jacket before she could grab hold of his arm and give it a hard shake. "Preston, are you okay?"

He paused, his eyes darting one direction and then the other.

"Pres, did you hear me? If you're too hot, let me help you get the jacket off."

He didn't move.

His words about being paralyzed came to mind. She gripped his elbow. "Preston, speak to me."

He startled and looked down at her. "Did you say something?"

"Yes, I asked if you were okay."

"I'm not sure." He replaced his jacket and straightened his tie without bothering to secure the shirt's top button. I'm going below. I'll see you when we dock."

As if shot from a cannon, he bolted across the deck to the steps.

Maureen stared after him until his boater disappeared from view, then glanced over the railing in time to see him open a door to the cabin and step inside. Should she go after him or was it best to give him time to collect himself? He'd been excited to take her on the steamship, but what joy could she have knowing he was troubled to the point of wanting to be inside? What happened to the Preston who'd always loved water and boats and anything connected to them? *Please, Lord, help me.*

PRESTON STEPPED into the stifling lower deck cabin, not surprised to find it almost empty except for a few elderly couples standing by the windows. The last thing he wanted was to look out at the water. He sat on a wooden bench at the middle of the room and rested his elbows on his knees. Why did he think taking the steamship was a good idea? Because Maureen would love it and he wanted to prove he was over this crazy stuff about being on the water. That his nightmares that made him relive that awful day over and over would stop.

He grew up on the water, and never was afraid of anything, even the worst storms. But standing at the railing a few minutes ago, he made the mistake of glancing down. In his mind he saw the churning water from the deck of the schooner and imagined a boy falling overboard. He was ready to take off his jacket and dive in when Maureen got his attention and he stopped, his arm half out of his coat. Seeing the horror on her face was all he could take, and he bolted. He was supposed to be her protector, not the other way around.

The door to the outer deck opened and he cringed and

averted his gaze. Why did she follow him? Without looking, he sensed she'd sat on the bench beside him. She took his hand and squeezed. She was too good for him. He'd get through the rest of today, and hopefully tomorrow, then he'd have to tell her the truth.

THE BOAT PULLED up to the exposition's dock, and Maureen sighed in relief. If Preston squeezed her hand any tighter it would have been flattened. "Pres, we're here and need to get off the boat."

He didn't move.

She drew in a breath and spoke in a firm tone. "Preston Stevens, please let go of my hand so we can get off this boat."

He startled and looked at her, his eyes wide. "Oh. Sorry. I was lost in thought." He released her then stood and gave her a tight smile. "Shall we?"

Telling herself to not question anything, she took his offered elbow and they worked themselves into the line of excited fair attendees. Back on shore, they stepped under a welcome-to-the-Columbian-Exposition sign that straddled the width of the pier and climbed several steps to a ticket booth.

Seeming normal again, Preston paid for the entry tickets and they headed toward the entrance behind others who had been on the boat with them. At the end of the Peristyle, a grand edifice made up of forty-eight columns representing the states and territories, they stepped between two of the columns and into the fairgrounds.

All concerns about Preston's odd behavior faded as she transitioned from concerned girlfriend to Alice at the bottom of the rabbit hole. Dazzling in the sun, glittering and white, larger-than-life buildings encircled a lagoon filled with sky-blue water. She'd read the buildings weren't really made of crystals, but it was easy to convince herself they were. The lagoon's water, calm, serene and peaceful, invited her to sit at the edge of the deck and quiet her soul. She pointed at a structure on the other side of the basin, "What is that gigantic building?"

Preston glanced at a map he'd purchased when he bought the tickets. "The Manufacturers and Liberal Arts Building. Definitely one I want to see. How are we to decide what to look at first?"

"I don't know. But I want to end the evening with a ride on the Ferris wheel. I hear the view of the lights at night is amazing."

"I read there's a new product called pancake mix. All the ingredients are together in one box, and all you need to do is add egg and water. They're giving away free pancakes. I think it's in this building right behind us. "Preston gestured toward the large Agricultural Building. Let's find that first."

She'd never eaten pancakes for lunch or supper before, but if the thought of doing so pushed the darkness out of his eyes, she'd eat them at midnight. "Pancakes sound wonderful. I think I'm hungry enough to eat a couple dozen."

They stepped inside the mammoth structure, and Pres stopped a man heading for the exit. "Excuse me, can you direct us to the pancake demonstration?"

The man grinned and gestured in the direction he'd just come from. "Go that way. When you see the line, you'll know you're in the right spot."

They headed down the wide aisle past people of all ages and ethnicities in all manner of dress. "There's a large gathering up ahead." Maureen picked up her pace. "That must be the place."

They came to a stop behind a couple and Preston asked if it was the line for pancakes.

The woman nodded. "Yes. This is the second time we've come. You won't be disappointed."

Hungry as she was, Maureen didn't want to spend most of

their time in line for some kind of instant pancake she might not like. "How long is the wait?"

"It goes quite fast." the woman offered a soft smile and looked at Maureen. "I'm Pauline Hudson."

"Maureen Quinn," She stuck out her hand and the lady took it then focused on Preston. "And this is Mr. Quinn, I presume."

Maureen's cheeks heated. "Oh, we're not married. He's Preston Stevens."

The woman blushed. "I'm so sorry."

Maureen waved her hand. "No problem. We're longtime friends."

Preston laughed. "I hope by now we're more than that."

Startled, she stared at him. "I guess we are."

Behind them a baby fussed and Maureen turned. A young woman balanced her baby on one arm while using the other to search in the large bag she carried.

"Here, let me hold your boy, if that would help."

The woman looked up at Maureen. "Oh, thank you so much. I have a snack for him somewhere in my bag." She handed Maureen the baby.

She bounced the child, that she presumed to be seven or eight months old, and spoke baby talk to him. He stared at her, his blue eyes seeming to take in all her features. Then, without warning, he sneezed. Tiny droplets sprayed over her face and she recoiled but worked to keep a smile on her face.

The mother took the boy back. "Alex, shame on you for sneezing on the nice lady." She looked at Maureen. "I'm so sorry."

Maureen took a handkerchief from her skirt pocket and blotted it over her face, wishing she had a basin of soap and water. "No problem. Babies have no idea of what's right and proper. I'm okay. She turned back, and Pres whispered in her ear. "Are you really okay?"

"Yes. I'm fine." She hoped their whispers weren't overheard by the mother.

They made small talk with the Hudsons until they were at the front of the line, and a young lady handed a plate of four pancakes to Maureen. "The syrup and butter are over at those tables." She pointed to their left.

They stopped at the table the woman pointed out and Maureen picked up a clean knife from a basket and sliced off a chunk of butter from a slab resting on a saucer. She spread it over the still-warm pancakes. As the butter began to melt, she drizzled syrup from one of the ceramic pitchers nearby.

By the time Maureen sat at a table Preston had secured in front of the demonstration, her stomach was growling. She spread a napkin on her lap and forked a bit of pancake into her mouth. The sweetness of the molasses and richness of the butter mingled with the fluffy cake on her tongue and tasted wonderful. She swallowed and took another bite. "These are the best pancakes I've ever tasted. I'm glad we stayed in line."

Preston took a mouthful and nodded. "I agree. I wonder if this mix can be purchased somewhere."

She bit into another morsel. "If not, it should be." She looked around for the young mother but couldn't spot her. "I should have washed up first, but now I need to find a public restroom and wash my face and hands."

They found a restroom then wandered the exhibits in the hall before they stepped outside. A gondola skimmed past them on the lagoon. A young couple snuggled together at one end while a man piloted the vessel with a long pole. Maureen grinned, imagining how wonderful it would be to snuggle with Pres the same way. "I'd love to take a gondola ride. Can we?"

He stiffened. "You just had a steamboat ride. Isn't that enough boating for one day?"

She scowled. Where did the happy man of a few minutes ago

disappear to? "A gondola is hardly the same as a steamboat. What's going on, Pres? You love boats and water, yet you seem to be trying to avoid them as much as possible."

A pained expression took over his features and he stared at his feet. "I'll explain later. Let's walk around to the other side and find the wooded island. I hear there's a magnificent Japanese display there, and according to the map, the women's building is nearby. I know you'll enjoy that."

Hours later, Maureen held Preston's arm as they walked up to the giant Ferris wheel on the Midway Plaisance under a sky that had been transformed into brilliant oranges and reds. They'd just made their way past what seemed to be an exhibit of all the misfits of the world, the most shocking of all, the scantily clad women gyrating around a small stage. She was all for women wearing pants when the occasion demanded it, or a swimming costume that allowed for freedom to actually swim, but to wear as little clothing as possible, exposing parts that only a husband should be privileged to see? Absolutely not.

While Preston bought their tickets, she stood back and tipped her head, letting her gaze follow the wheel past its compartments, which were as large as train cars, jammed with people, to the very top. As much as she wanted to see the view of the fair and beyond from the up there, was it really safe? It had been operating since June without a reported mishap. Surely, she could trust it.

Preston approached. "What do you think? You still want to ride the wheel?"

Never would she let him see her fear. She pushed a smile to her face. "Of course. I've always wanted to be up high and be able to look down. Now's my chance."

"Ah, my fearless woman. Since you couldn't fly using your bicycle, now is your opportunity. Your wish is my command."

Her stomach flipped at his calling her his woman, but she wasn't so sure about the fearless part.

Soon they were ushered into one of the cars. Her stomach fluttering with anticipation of the thrill of being up so high next to the man in her life, Maureen sat next to one of the windows that faced the east.

"You sure you don't want to sit on the other side?"

She stared at Preston. His weird behavior was emerging again. "Of course not. Nothing to see over there. I want to see the fairgrounds and the lake beyond."

"Guess you're right." He sighed and sat beside her, then settled his arm over her shoulders. Like before, she felt tension emanating from his hand through the fabric of her shirtwaist. The wheel started moving, rose up a short distance, then stopped to load the car below them. After several more stops they arrived at the top. Dusk had settled over the area like a soft blanket and the fairgrounds below shone bright, almost like how she envisioned heaven—white, glowing and welcoming. Beyond the fair, out on the lake, a lone light shone from what was probably the steamer they rode on earlier. "Pres isn't it beautiful. It's like a fairyland."

He tugged her into his side until she nestled under his arm. "Not as beautiful as you, Mo." With his free hand he nudged her under her chin to turn her face toward him and kissed her. She kissed him back and they held the kiss until the wheel started turning. As romantic as it was to kiss at the top, his kiss was lifeless.

She wanted to grab him and kiss him with as much passion as she could muster to wake up the man who kissed her that afternoon in the depot. Instead, she leaned back and kept her gaze on his silhouette. "Pres, what's bothering you?"

He removed his arm from her shoulder. "Nothing. Let's enjoy the ride."

"If you think I'm going to believe you, you're wrong. We've been friends for too long."

He folded his arms across his chest. "It's nothing."

She faced the window as they whizzed past the bottom and began the ascent to the top. The sign at the ticket booth said three revolutions. They had one more after this one. Before he took her home, she'd get him to talk.

66

CHAPTER EIGHT

aureen followed Preston off the Ferris wheel. He took her hand and led her away from the ride. "We're close to the train stop. Why don't we go home by rail, rather than the steamboat?"

Her heart sank. He was slipping back into that mysterious state of mind again. She'd been looking forward to a moonlight cruise no matter how short it would be, and she wasn't about to give up. "I'd prefer the steamship."

He stiffened and let her hand drop. "No. We'll take the train."

Stunned at his brusqueness, she swallowed the growing lump in her throat. "Pres, I was looking forward to the steamship. Why don't you want to take the boat?"

"We are taking the train."

He retook her hand in a not-so-gentle way and pulled her in the direction of the train.

She had to almost run to keep up with his long strides. "This will cost you more since we already have the return ticket for the boat."

"I know."

Maureen blinked back tears. He was not the same man she'd

known all her life. Something was terribly wrong. They arrived at the platform, and within a few minutes a train arrived. Settled next to him on their seat she kept her face turned away as the inky blackness of the city outside the window seemed darker than usual after the bright lights of the Exposition.

"Maureen, I'm sorry. I have no idea what came over me."

She faced him. "I don't know either, Preston, but something isn't right. Please tell me what happened. This has something to do with that storm doesn't it?"

He nodded. "After we get to our stop, we'll talk."

They rode in silence until they arrived at Wilmette. Back on the sidewalk, Preston offered his arm. "There's a park a couple of blocks down. We can sit on one of the benches."

After two blocks of excruciating silence, they settled on a secluded bench not far from the street.

Preston sighed. "I don't know where to start."

"Try the beginning."

"The storm was worse than any storm I'd been through on Geneva Lake, but I found it exciting to take the surf boat out to a schooner that was in trouble. I'd trained for moments like these and was a good swimmer. All people on the boat were men except for a young woman and her son about four years old. They were the wife and son of one of the sailors. We used a rope to connect to the distressed vessel and got all the crew off. We didn't realize the mother and her boy were on board until we'd already rescued the crew. I volunteered to go to the schooner for them. I helped the mother get across while I stayed with the boy. After she was safe on the surf boat, I secured the boy to me and we started across the rope."

He paused and drew in a breath "The wind was horrible and the waves were nearly touching my feet. I've never seen anything like it. We were only about 20 feet from the surf boat when the boy let go of my neck and slid into the water. I went in after him and dove and dove but the churning water was murky. In my groping, I finally felt him and dragged him to the surface. We were pulled into the surf boat. His mother screamed at me that it was my fault her boy had drowned. Then her husband joined her accusations.

"She was right. It was my fault. We got back to shore, and I refused to believe he was gone and tried to give the boy artificial respiration, until I was pulled off his body." A sob exploded and he wiped his face with his sleeve. "He didn't make it. I went straight to bed. When I finally slept, I dreamed I was still in the water and could see the boy. I'd reach out to him, but he was always too far away." His voice broke. "I'm a murderer as much as if I'd pulled a trigger and shot that boy. That woman's screams are constantly in my head now.

Maureen reached out to hug him, but he pushed her away.

"I haven't gone on any rescues since then, and that's why I was told to take a few days off. They're hoping when I get back on Monday I'll be my old self. But nothing has changed. I can't do my job anymore. I'm short-tempered and hardly sleep. And I'm sure you've noticed I lose patience with people. I need to resign. I don't know what I'll do or where I'll go after that." He faced her and took her hand. "Maureen, we've been best friends since we learned to walk, and I've always loved you. But I can't see you anymore. I'm afraid one day my anger will get the best of me and I'll hurt you. Please forgive me."

She couldn't believe what she was hearing. Surely time would take care of this. "No. Preston, I'm not going to let you send me away. People who love each other stick together."

He released her hand by flinging it away and leaned back. "I can't be with you. Why can't you accept the truth?"

Her voice rose above his. "Because I care about you, Preston Stevens. Why can't you get it through that thick skull of yours?"

He wrapped his arms around her and pressed his face on her shoulder. A sob came from his throat. This was really bad, but he needed her, and she wasn't going away. He leaned back. In the darkness she couldn't see his eyes, but she was certain her own couldn't look any worse than his. "Maybe after a good night's sleep and another day at the fair, you'll feel better."

"I can't return to the fair tomorrow. I could barely get through today. I need to return to Michigan and turn in my notice, and you need to go your own way. Maybe you and Sophie can attend the fair together before you go home."

A lump pressed against her throat, and she swallowed against it. This was really the end. "No. If I can't go to the fair again with you, I don't want to go at all. I'll probably go back to Lake Geneva."

He drew her into a hug. "I'm so sorry, Mo. You are too good for me." He brought his lips to hers. She pulled him closer and kissed him hard. He broke the kiss then he trailed kisses over her face to her ear and kissed it, sending warm goosebumps down her neck. She wanted him in ways she'd never wanted a man before. Their mouths found each other again and the kiss deepened until breathless, they parted.

She chuckled. "For a man who just told me you want to break up you sure know how to kiss goodbye."

"I don't want to break up, Mo. You know that. But until I'm better it's best we not be together." He stood then took her hand and drew her to her feet. "I'll walk you to Sophie's."

CHAPTER NINE

*P*reston jammed his hands in his trouser pockets and walked in the direction of his family's home. Staring at his feet as he walked, he whispered, "God, what's wrong with me. I care so much for Maureen, but I'm afraid to be with her. It took all I had to stop myself from belting her across her mouth when she persisted we take the steamboat back. I've never hit a woman. I used to think life was all fun and frivolity. Not any longer. I'm no good to anyone. Not Maureen, not my dad or mother or the rest of the family. I can't even save a little boy!"

He arrived at his house but continued walking until he reached Lake Michigan. He came to a narrow stretch of sand and plopped down. A full moon gleamed near the horizon. Was this what his life was going to be from now on? He just said goodbye to the most important woman in his life, and he couldn't do the job he loved anymore or the one he always dreamed of having on Geneva Lake. When his family finds out how he failed to save the boy, shame will be brought on them. There was only one answer. He unlaced his shoes and pulled off his socks, then rolled up his pants legs.

At the water's edge, the cool water tickled his toes. Already anxiety had mounted, and fear was creeping in. Although the water was calm, he couldn't look at it without seeing churning waves. He stepped in and waded through the water, until it lapped at his knees. How long would it be before he'd be missed? Mo wouldn't be looking for him. His family didn't even know he was here. He supposed when he didn't show up back at the station, they'd start a search. Giving himself to the lake was an apt punishment for his failure at saving the boy. He walked in farther. His body was getting numb in the cold water. A couple more steps and it would all be over.

MAUREEN STEPPED into Sophie's home grateful no one was waiting up to greet her. The last she needed was to act like nothing was wrong when all she wanted was to crawl in bed and cry herself to sleep. She climbed the stairs, careful to step around the spot halfway up where a board creaked and tiptoed to her room.

She'd just slipped her nightgown over her head when a knock came at the door. She startled. "Who is it?"

The door opened and Sophie stuck her head in. "Who else would it be but me? How was the fair?"

Mo looked away. "Okay."

"Just okay?"

She faced Sophie, and the tears she'd held back broke through. Sophie came across the room and threw her arms around Maureen.

"It was awful. Something is terribly wrong with Preston, and he broke up with me." She pressed her face into Sophie's shoulder unable to stop the sobs.

With her arms around her, Sophie walked Maureen over to the bed where they both sat. "What do you mean something is wrong with him?"

"I don't know how to explain it. He told me about a terrible thing that happened during a rescue and he can't shake it off. He's having nightmares and mood changes and is actually afraid of the water. He's always loved the water and boats, and now he can't stand to be near either one. He's afraid he'll hurt me if he suddenly gets angry, so we're not seeing each other anymore." She wiped her nose with the back of her hand.

Sophie pulled a handkerchief from her robe pocket and handed it to her.

Maureen dabbed her eyes. "I'm returning to Lake Geneva tomorrow."

"Where is Preston going?"

"Back to Manitou Island so he can officially quit the service. After that I have no idea. I told him that surely in time he'll get over this, but he doesn't think so."

"Do you think this is an act for a way to break up with you?"

"Not the way he kissed me a few minutes ago. That's what hurts so much. I'm thinking eventually he'll have to come back to Geneva Lake. I plan to be there when he does."

"Maybe before you go to the train depot tomorrow you should go over to his house and make sure he's okay."

Mo wiped the moisture from her cheeks. "I'll see. There's only one train that leaves for Traverse City and that's midafternoon. He might be there."

The next morning, Maureen was up before seven, having not slept but a couple of hours all night. She packed her bag, then left it at Sophie's and walked the six blocks to Preston's home, hoping the fresh air would clear her head.

She arrived at the Tudor-style house and climbed the seven or eight steps to the front door and yanked on the chain. A tinkling of bells sounded from the other side of the door. A minute later she yanked again several times in succession. Since the family was at Lake Geneva for the summer, most of their household help had gone there with them. The few that didn't go were released to find work elsewhere. If he had as restless a night as she, he might still be asleep.

She yanked at the bell cord again.

"You lookin' for someone?"

She spun around and stared at a man standing on the walk, a garden hoe in his hand. "Yes. Preston Stevens. Have you seen him this morning?"

"No ma'am. He was here the last day or two. I'm the gardener next door. Haven't seen him this morning though."

Her heart fell. Maybe he left early to wait for his train downtown. "Thanks."

"You want me to tell him who was callin' for him if I see him?"

She shook her head. "Thanks, but no."

The man walked toward the property next door, and she started out for Sophie's. It was probably better this way. She'd see him again whenever he turned up at the lake.

CHAPTER TEN

*P*reston stirred and tried to straighten his legs but couldn't. He felt beneath his back, then under his head. The small pillow was flatter than those pancakes at the fair. Where in the world was he? He forced his eyes open and pushed up on one arm to survey the dank small space. His gaze halted at a wall of bars. He closed his eyes and opened them again. The bars were still there. He pushed himself into a sitting position on what appeared to be a narrow cot, then focused on a similar cot on the other side of the cell.

A slovenly looking man sat on the edge of the narrow bed staring at him. "Bout time you woke up. You've been sleeping ever since they brought you here last night."

He rubbed his eyes and worked to clear his mind as jumbled memories crashed into his brain. The night at the fair with Maureen, their passionate kiss, breaking up with her, and walking into Lake Michigan. He wasn't supposed to be here, he was supposed to be in hell where he deserved to be. He sat up. "Where am I?"

"Bridewell Jail. They don't call it that anymore. Got a fancier name now, but it's still the same Cook County Jail where all us bad guys go until we have our day in court."

He winced. "What did I do to land here?"

His cellmate chuckled. "If you don't know, I sure don't. Now that you're awake maybe he can tell you." He pointed to a man in a crisp blue uniform who was unlocking the cell.

The officer stepped in and stared at Preston. "Sleeping Beauty is awake I see. Now maybe you can tell us what your name is."

Pres rubbed his head. "Not until I know what I did to be here."

"You don't know?"

He shook his head. My brain's a little foggy. Something tells me I need to get a lawyer before I say anything."

The cop rolled his eyes. "I'll be back." He let himself out of the cell and the door slammed behind him with a loud *clink*.

Pres faced the man on the cot. "So now what happens?"

"You got a lawyer to call?"

"Yeah, I know one but he's more a business lawyer than a courtroom one."

"That's more of a start than most of us have."

A few minutes later, the policeman returned and Preston gave him his name and the name of Stuart Ferguson, their company's lawyer. While they were talking, a guard came for the cellmate, and soon Preston was alone. He hadn't even asked the man's name.

He lay down and stretched out as best he could, facing the wall. Hopefully Ferguson could at least arrange bail. So far as he knew, suicide wasn't against the law. What a failure he was. He couldn't even kill himself right. Hopefully, Dad wouldn't stop Ferguson from bailing him out. This was probably the last straw as far as his father was concerned. At least once Maureen heard about this, it would cool any feelings she still had for him. It was a good thing he broke it off with her last night. The last he'd want was for her to see him in this hovel. He let himself drift off. At least asleep he didn't have to feel or think.

"Stevens, wake up your lawyer is here. Let's go."

Preston opened his eyes and sat up with a jerk, nearly falling off the cot. He blinked at the cop standing at the cell door. He grabbed up his jacket where it lay in a crumbled heap on the floor and hustled to the uniformed man.

The policeman opened the cell door far enough for Preston to step through, then closed it. "Follow me."

After walking through a series of hallways, the policeman opened a door. "You're to wait in here."

Preston stepped into a small room barren except for a wooden table and a couple of chairs. He walked to a tiny window that cast the only light in the space. Two floors down, people—some uniformed cops and others in plain clothes—scurried up to the entrance while others came out, walking at a slower pace. He'd never heard of this jail, but as much as he could tell it wasn't located downtown. He looked off in the direction of the fair. What a contrast to the gaiety and glitz of the grounds this was. One day, enjoying pancakes and riding the Ferris wheel with his girl and the next, waking up in a musty jail cell. The door opened behind him and he turned.

Except for his graying temples, Stuart Ferguson hadn't changed since Preston had last seen him three years ago at Dad's office. Wearing a dark suit and tie, he set a leather case on the table. "Sit, Preston."

He settled on the wooden chair across from the attorney. "Thanks for coming. Can you get me out of here?"

"Yes. But before we leave, we need to talk. To begin, all charges have been dropped, since you didn't break the law by sleeping on the beach. At first, they thought you were another man the police are looking for, but now that they know you aren't, you're free to go. I understand you claim you have no memory of being brought here. You were only a mile from your home. What were you doing on the beach?"

Preston shook his head. "It's a long story. I honestly don't know how I ended up sleeping on the beach. The last memory I have is walking into the water determined to end my life."

Ferguson's eyes widened. "That doesn't sound like you. Whatever happened?"

He gave him a short version of the past several weeks, then said, "I need help but I have no idea if anyone will believe me or understand. He slumped against the chair. I suppose my parents know about this."

"Yes. I spoke to your father just before I came here. He wants you to go to Lake Geneva on the next train. It's best you get out of the city as soon as possible. I'll get my driver to take you to the station."

Preston stared down at his rumpled shirt and trousers. "Can't I at least go back to the house for a change of clothes? I look like a bum. And what about my position with the life saving station? I'm due back there by midnight tomorrow."

"It is all taken care of. You won't be returning. As of today, you are formally discharged from your duties. I took the liberty of stopping by your house on the way here and found your grip. I'll get it for you." He stood and left the room.

Preston stared at the window. Maybe a few nights in jail would have been better than facing his father. How long would it be before he was evicted from Shelter Bay and the Wilmette house?

Ferguson stepped into the room carrying Preston's suitcase. "Let's get you changed. The next train to Lake Geneva leaves in an hour.

MAUREEN ARRIVED at the train depot minutes before the Lake Geneva train was due to depart. She scurried up the stairs and stepped through the door, pushing away the memory of Preston spinning her around and kissing her in that very room. It was only yesterday, but it seemed more like a year. She made a beeline to the passenger trains and found the one she wanted. A porter approached and offered to carry her suitcase and they boarded the train. She started to sit in the first available aisle seat and came to an abrupt halt, almost causing the porter to run into her.

Preston was in the window seat. At least, it looked like him. Hard to tell, though, by his disheveled appearance. "What are you doing here?"

He winced and faced the window. "I imagine I'm going the same place you are."

She glanced at the porter. "I'll be sitting here." She handed him a couple of coins and he set her bag on the floor in front of the seat. She sat beside Preston and rearranged her skirt. "I suppose I should not have sat here, but there's hardly an empty seat available. I thought you were supposed to return to Michigan."

"I was able to quit by telephone. I'm not going back."

She took in the whole of him, running her gaze over his grizzled jaw and rumpled hair. While his shirt and trousers were clean, the rest of him looked like he'd been on a bender. "Have a rough night?"

"You could say that. But it's not what you're thinking."

"Then what happened?"

"Too long a story."

She sniffed, No alcohol odor. If it wasn't that what was it? "I had a bad night also. Couldn't sleep because someone I love dearly decided he doesn't want me in his life anymore."

"That's too bad. You should listen to that person. If he doesn't want you around, then it's best you leave him alone."

"I don't think it's accidental that we're on the same train. Maybe we're meant to talk things out. We have the next two hours."

He squirmed and peered at her with inexpressive eyes. Her heart squeezed. Maybe he was right to break up with her. She looked away. "Since it pleases you so much, I'll be out of your life as soon as we arrive in Lake Geneva."

They rode most of the way in agonizing silence. A sullen Preston stared out the window, and she sat with arms folded across her chest, torn between wanting to shake him and demand he tell her what went on last night and yearning to wrap her arms around him and comfort him.

The train hissed to a halt at the Lake Geneva depot and she stood and reached for her suitcase.

Preston's hand landed on top of hers. "I'll get that for you, Mo."

She ignored the familiar tingles rushing up her arm and pulled her hand away. "Thank you."

They walked single file down the aisle, Preston managing both their suitcases, and stepped onto the platform. Across the way, Da stood next to Horace Stevens, who looked almost as worse for wear as his son. Wonderful. By the looks on their faces, it was clear they both knew more than she did about the situation.

Next to her, Preston groaned. "We're both in trouble now if those two have been talking."

"Agreed." They approached the men, each going to their respective father.

Da nodded at Preston then gathered Maureen into a hug. "Glad you're back. Let's get you home." He picked up her suitcase that Preston had set on the ground and put it in the phaeton then helped Maureen into her seat. He got the horse heading toward Main Street and home.

They traveled in silence for a few minutes then Da spoke.

"It's nice having a road to the property now so we don't have to always go by boat."

"I always enjoyed the short boat ride," Maureen said. "Soothing after the two-hour train trip."

"I suppose, but I have a feeling no boat ride will soothe you enough today. Horace told me what happened with Preston last night."

She snapped her gaze his direction. "What happened? He wouldn't tell me."

"I presumed you knew since you took the train together."

"We broke up last night. I had no idea he'd be on the train today. I thought he was heading back to Manitou Station. Da, he's been acting strangely the past two days. He said he's afraid if he continues to see me, he'll cause me harm because he can't control his anger."

By the time Da pulled the carriage into Safe Refuge, Maureen had heard what Pres had refused to tell her. She dabbed her eyes with her handkerchief. "Please, let's not say anything to Mama. She already dislikes Preston, and this will only make it worse. Before that boat disaster, he'd changed and matured. He wanted to start a boat building business, and we were going to live here at the lake. Now our dreams have crumbled."

He halted the carriage and looked at her. "Don't give up yet, Maureen. I have a sense time will heal this. I can't imagine how he must feel having lost that little boy in the water."

She nodded. "I understand why he didn't tell me what happened to him last night. How awful to wake up in a jail cell. What if he'd succeeded in killing himself?"

He draped his arm over her shoulders and pulled her next to him. "He didn't succeed, and the fact he woke up on the beach shows he must have changed his mind and left the water of his own accord. We'll not think about that anymore. Let's get inside and get you to bed. You look exhausted."

"Thanks for understanding, Da." She climbed out of the carriage and walked with her father to the house.

Mama opened the door before they reached it. She grabbed Maureen by the elbow and tugged her inside. "I'm relieved you are okay. I could give that Preston Stevens a piece of my mind for leading you on like he did."

"Mama, he didn't lead me on. He's not well right now. Let's leave it at that. I just want to sleep the rest of the day. Maybe when I'm more rested we can talk."

Mama looked at Da. "Say something to her."

"Anna, Horace was at the station to meet Preston. They were both on the same train. There's a lot more to the story than we knew before. She's right. Preston isn't well."

"What do you mean not well?" She looked at Maureen. "What has he exposed you to?"

"It's not anything she can catch, sweetheart. It's up to her to tell you the rest. I'll get the phaeton to the carriage house and the horse turned out."

Mama threw up her hands. "All right. I just don't want to see our daughter hurt."

"Nor do I." He took her into his arms. "But we can't protect our fledglings forever. You know that."

Maureen turned toward the stairs, not wanting to see her parents kissing. She loved hearing the story of how they had met and, years later, they still acted like newlyweds, but not today. In her bedroom, she slipped out of her clothes, letting them pool on the floor. She dropped a clean nightgown over her head then plucked the pins out of her up-do and let her hair fall past her shoulders. She crossed to the bed, picked up a pillow, and pressed it to her mouth, stifling the scream that pushed against her throat.

Right then all she wanted to do was sleep. It was the only way to escape this nightmare.

CHAPTER ELEVEN

Two Weeks Later

Maureen drew a handkerchief from her handbag and blotted her face. The cool September air had felt good as it drifted in through the open windows, yet now Alice's living room was hotter than an oven. She returned the hanky to her bag and focused on Mrs. Seymour, the mayor's wife, who was speaking about forming study groups the same way their friend, Reanette McCray, was doing in Chicago. Maureen blinked and stifled a yawn. She was sure the groups were a wonderful way to enlighten people to the need for women to vote, but right then all she wanted was to go home to bed.

"Then it's all settled. Angela will begin working on a schedule for the groups, and Harriet will line up homes where the groups will gather. We'll meet back here in two weeks at nine a.m. Meeting is adjourned."

Maureen rested her head against the cushioned chair back and willed herself to gather enough energy to stand. Just a few more minutes and surely it would come.

"Maureen. Maureen. Wake up."

Someone was shaking her shoulder.

She opened her eyes and stared into Alice's concerned face. "I'm sorry. I didn't mean to drift off."

Alice rested her hand against Maureen's forehead. "Good heavens, Mo. You're burning up. It can't be an infection from the tooth extraction. It's been too long, and when I checked the socket last week, it was completely closed over. Wait here. I'll be right back."

Maureen blinked and yawned. She hadn't felt ill this morning when she rode her bicycle to the meeting. But now she doubted she had the strength to ride it home.

Alice reappeared wearing a medical mask over her nose and mouth. "Don't be alarmed. With a small child, I have to be careful. Until the doctor examines you, it's wise to be cautious."

What on earth did Alice think she had? "It can't be more than a bad cold, can it?"

Her friend paused. "I'd rather keep my suspicions to myself. It's probably that. I'll take you home in my carriage. We can store your bicycle in the space behind the seats. I've already called your mother and told her you've taken ill. She's waiting for us."

Maureen gripped the chair arms and pushed on them to stand. She made it to her feet but wobbled and fell back into the chair. "Can't we go by Doctor Kiley's on the way so he can check me?"

"Doctor Murphy has taken over Doctor Kiley's practice now. But at present he's delivering a baby. I already checked. I left word for him to come to your home later. He's very nice and a good doctor."

"I'm already acquainted with him through church. How did I get so weak?"

"It's the fever. Come on, I'll help you stand. It's a good thing my husband is home this morning and the baby is napping. He's hitching the horse to the carriage now."

By the time the women turned into the drive leading to Safe Refuge, it was all Maureen could do to keep her eyes open. Alice brought the horse to a halt. "Both your parents are waiting for you. Wait here a moment."

Maureen nodded and gave in to her heavy eyelids.

"Do we really need to wear masks?" Da's voice rose above the softer ones belonging to Alice and Mama.

"Yes. As a precaution. I checked her mouth and there are no sores as yet, but with the other symptoms I fear they are coming. I hope it's not what I think, but it's best to be safe. Did you consider where she might rest comfortably without passing it to anyone else?"

"Yes." There was Da's voice again. "The cottage over there will work. Our older daughter is living there now, but she can move over here."

Maureen's eyes popped open. Why was she going to Katie's cottage?

Before she could ask or give her opinion on the decision, Da was lifting her out of the carriage. "Let's go my *A Stor*, and get you settled."

Da hadn't called her his treasure like that since she was a child. She wrapped her arms around his neck the way she used to do and her hand fell on a bow. She forced her eyes open and stared at the white mask over half his face. "Am I so sick you need a mask too?"

"Mrs. Barber thinks you might be. You'll be staying in the cottage so you don't pass on to us whatever you have. Katie will move into the main house."

"I can't be that sick. Katie shouldn't have to move."

"It's best to be careful. She'll be moving out in a few more weeks anyway after the wedding."

"Where's Mama?

"I'm right here, Maureen. I've got a fresh nightgown for you. Doctor Murphy is on his way."

A memory of the handsome ginger-haired doctor who sat next to her at church a couple of weeks ago broke through the fog. Mama had presumed they were together that Sunday and strongly suggested she get to know the eligible doctor. Mama had thought him a far better match for her than Preston.

Maureen pressed her face against Da's jacket. "I don't need a doctor. I only need to sleep. I'll be better in a few days." *Why don't they understand? All I need is sleep.*

NATE MURPHY WALKED across the flagstone path to the two-story house Mr. Quinn referred to as "the cottage." It was a lot nicer than any cottage he'd ever seen. He expected the man of the house to greet him wearing the latest fashion men of means usually wore when they were at their lake homes, but this man wore work dungarees and a long-sleeved cotton work shirt.

"I hate that my wife and I aren't allowed inside with our daughter, but we're grateful to have been able to hire Beatrice Ambrose on short notice to be her round-the-clock caretaker," Mr. Quinn said.

Nate said a silent prayer of thanks that Bea was available. "I can't think of anyone finer to care for your daughter. Having had smallpox herself, she knows what her patients are going through."

"I couldn't help but notice the scarring on her face. Is that what we can expect for Maureen?"

"Every case is different. Only time will tell."

Mr. Quinn stopped a few feet from the entrance to the cottage. "This is as far as I can go, Doctor. Ring the door chimes on the main house's door after you've examined her. Mrs. Quinn and I will wait there."

Nate nodded then took the last couple of steps to the door, lifted the brass knocker and rapped several times.

The door opened, and Bea Ambrose greeted him with a smile that caused the creases around her blue eyes to deepen. She wore her usual caretaker uniform of a plain gray dress to her ankles and a white pinafore with huge pockets bulging with items she liked to keep handy. "Nate Murphy. Someday we'll have to meet under better circumstances rather than because of someone's illness. We've been waiting for you."

"Hello, Bea. Sorry I couldn't get here sooner. The baby was breech and it was a difficult delivery."

"We understand. Come in."

"Not until I dress." He pulled a medical mask from his bag and tied it in place, making sure it fully covered his mouth, nose and beard, then stepped into a small entryway. "Where is our patient?"

She pointed to a closed door. "She's set up on a bed in there. It's normally a study of sorts but for now it's an infirmary. We have indoor plumbing and the bathroom is right around the corner. We are also blessed with electric. If you need to use a telephone there is none here, but there's one in the main house in the kitchen. Their oldest daughter teaches school and is gone during the day. Mrs. Quinn or their teenage son will always be home. There's also another daughter who looks to be eight or nine years old. Mr. Quinn is a landscaper and owns and operates a florist and landscaping business and is in and out. None of the family has been vaccinated, but are not showing symptoms. I suggest they get vaccinated right away. I think Maureen is awake now. If you'd like to go in."

"You're certain she has smallpox?"

"You have to officially declare it, but she's manifesting all the symptoms. She and a friend attended the Columbian Exposition a couple of weeks ago, and she probably was exposed there. The friend has not come down with it, but Maureen told me that while at the fair, she held a baby for his mother, and the baby sneezed into her face. She has no idea of the mother's name or where she lives to follow up."

Nate pulled a notebook and pencil from his case and noted what Bea had related. "Sounds like a possible source. I'll go in now." He tapped lightly on the door and heard a weak "come in."

He opened the door and looked toward the bed, but all he saw was a fluffy comforter. Somewhere beneath it was his new patient. "Miss Quinn, I'm Doctor Murphy. I'll be examining you today, then checking on you several times a week."

"Mrs. Ambrose said you were coming."

He stepped closer and peered over the bed clothes. His jaw fell open. The same pretty girl who'd sold him his bedroom dresser, then a week later sat next to him at church. He'd regretted not getting her name at the furniture store, and she scooted away so fast after the service, he didn't have opportunity to ask. "And so, we meet again. First in the furniture store, then at church."

"This is the one place I'd have preferred not to meet. I'm fairly certain I wasn't yet exposed to this thing until after our chance meetings."

She scooted up against her pillows and focused her green eyes on him. "On both occasions I was struck at how much your red hair and beard remind me of my Da."

He scowled. "Your Da?"

"With a name like Murphy, I thought you'd know Irish children call their father *Da*. Da's hair and beard are graying now, but I remember when they looked much like yours."

He smiled. "So that means I can look at your father and have a good idea how I'll look when I reach his age. I was raised by my mother only. My father, who was Irish, died when I was a baby…" What was he doing, telling her his life story? He'd never done that before with a patient. At least not one he'd only met a short time ago. He opened his bag and pulled out a stethoscope.

"Your rash is likely smallpox, but I need to do an exam before I officially declare it."

"You mean my pock marks, don't you? I don't need you to soft-peddle the diagnosis. I can take the bad news without hysterics."

Nate stifled a chuckle. This woman had spunk. Perhaps it was best to not explain the spots weren't pock marks until after the infection left its calling card. He said a mental prayer the Lord would help him do his job as a doctor, despite feeling drawn to this woman from the moment he'd first laid eyes on her. The attraction so strong, he'd bought a piece of furniture he abhorred.

CHAPTER TWELVE

A jangling bell jarred Preston from his sleep. Someone was in trouble. He needed to get there, save the boy. He threw off the covers, planted his bare feet on the cold floor and looked about the room. Where were his dungarees? He blinked. It was only another one of those dreams.

But the bell still rang.

It was the telephone downstairs. He scooted across the floor to the staircase and scrambled down the stairs and toward the hall where the device had been installed several weeks ago. Someone must really want him to let it ring so long. He grabbed the earpiece.

"Shelter Bay. Hello."

"Preston, is that you?"

The voice was familiar. "Yes."

"This is Rory Quinn. Sorry to call at such an early hour but you should know Maureen is very ill."

His brain cleared and he straightened. "What? Where is she? How?"

"She's quarantined in our cottage. A woman who has already had smallpox and is immune is taking care of her. We thought you should know since you were with her in Chicago a few weeks ago. We think she may have caught it at the fair, but we're not sure. Are you feeling okay?"

Small Pox? People die from that. He willed his heart to slow down. "Yes. I'm fine. Can I see her?"

"I'm afraid not as she's very contagious. It will likely be a month before she's well. I'm glad to hear you are okay. I'd think if you were to catch it, you would have by now. How are you doing otherwise?"

What did it matter how he was doing? "I'm fine." *Physically anyway.* "Don't people die from smallpox?"

Silence fell on the connection. "Yes, sometimes they do, but with the care she's receiving from Mrs. Ambrose, we're assured she has a good chance of pulling through."

"Would it be all right to send her a note? Let her know I'm praying for her?"

"I think she'd like that, Preston."

They spoke a few more minutes and ended the call. He leaned against the wall. Was he really past the point of not coming down with it? He kissed her the night they broke up. And not just a peck on the cheek. He forced his mind back to the steamboat ride. She had stayed on the upper deck longer than he.

The first interaction they had with people that day was while they waited in line to have pancakes. He snapped his fingers. That was it. The baby sneezed on her. Her whole face was covered with his spray. She'd been worried about his germs and washed her face in the restroom. If she caught the smallpox from that baby's sneeze, that disease must be stronger than soap. Or had it already infected her before she went to the restroom?

Maureen was already upset with him for what he did to her, and now she probably blamed him for this, since it was his idea to attend the fair. But no, that wasn't how she was. Blaming him was something *he* would do.

He pushed away from the wall. He had no idea where Mom kept her stationery, but he'd tear the house apart until he found it.

An hour later, Preston sealed the envelope containing his note. The quickest way to get it to Mo was to drop it off at the house by boat. Could he do it? He stepped onto the veranda and stared down the slope to the dock where the *Ida* bobbed. Dad expected him to use the boat occasionally to keep the motor primed, but he'd not touched her since he had returned after the fair. If he took the *Ida*, he'd arrive at the Quinn's in ten minutes.

He took the four steps off the porch to the grass and crossed to the stairs that led down to the water. He arrived at the top step and halted. His legs refused to move. What was wrong with him? This wasn't Lake Michigan, and the water was calm with nary a cloud in the sky. How many trips had he made across the lake from Shelter Bay to Safe Refuge? Dozens. And now the thought of making the simple trip repulsed him.

He wouldn't let this control him. He lifted his foot and placed it on the first step, then the next. Each step came easier. At the bottom, he strode across the shore path and stopped where the pier met the shore. Only a few more steps, and he'd be at the *Ida*. He stared across the water at the Quinn's dock. If it weren't for the pine trees, he would be able to see the cottage where Mo lay sick— maybe dying. Moisture burned his eyes. What a man he turned out to be. So fearful he can't even take a simple boat ride to deliver a note to the girl he'd grown up with and had loved all his life.

He gripped the envelope at both ends and prepared to rip it apart.

What if she died and didn't know how much he cared about her? He had to take it to her, but he'd go by horseback. That he could do.

CHAPTER THIRTEEN

Three weeks later

Maureen woke, drenched in perspiration. She threw off her covers and goosebumps erupted. She needed a clean gown. She pushed herself into a sitting position and tried to swing her legs over the side of the bed. They may as well have been held down by a couple of anchors.

She fell against her pillows and blinked at the moisture stinging her eyes. It wasn't only her legs. Her entire body had been anchored to the bed for days, imprisoned in the cottage while everyone else's life had moved on without her. Katie's wedding was two weeks off. She was to be her maid of honor, and now Mary Lou Hobbs, her sister's best friend, had been enlisted as a backup. Her scabs had just begun to fall off, but she'd been told it could take a week before they were completely gone. Until then she was still contagious.

She reached over to the nightstand and picked up the bell to call for Mrs. Ambrose. If it weren't for her, Mama would have insisted on being her nursemaid. Mrs. Ambrose was an angel sent by God of that she was convinced, otherwise they'd probably be dealing with two invalids instead of one.

The bedroom door opened, and Mrs. Ambrose stepped in carrying folded sheets. "You woke just in time. These clean sheets are fresh from the line."

Maureen forced a weak smile. "I hope you have a clean nightgown too. I've drenched this one. I think my fever broke."

The older woman's face brightened. "Praise God. You are definitely on the mend."

"How long now until I'm well?"

"Probably another week. All the scabs need to come off."

"I was hoping you'd have a different answer." Maureen picked up the hand mirror from the nightstand and stared at her image. Scabs clustered her left cheek while the other stayed free of the horrible things. She blinked away her tears. "Well and marred for life." She snapped her mouth shut. "I'm so sorry. I should not be complaining. Especially not to you."

Mrs. Ambrose touched her fingertips to the pock marks that covered her own face. "Why not. It's only those like us who understand. At least you'll have scars only on part of your face."

Maureen harrumphed. "True, but I can't go through life keeping my good side toward people. It might work okay when having a photograph made, but not in real life." She set the mirror on the table and noticed an envelope. She picked it up and stared at the familiar handwriting. "How long has this letter been sitting here."

"A young man dropped it off some weeks ago while you were at your worst and sleeping most of the time. I told you it was there, but you only muttered something like he can't see you like this and I should take his letter away. We all say things we don't mean when we're delirious with fever. It's been in the nightstand drawer ever since. I took it out today."

"I'm afraid in this case, I do mean it. It doesn't matter. The relationship ended before I took ill."

"Do you want me to take the letter away?"

She pressed her lips together. She'd hardly given Preston a thought in weeks. When she wasn't sleeping and Doctor Murphy was there, they'd end up talking about all sorts of things. He never stopped surprising her with all he was interested in. And when Doctor Murphy wasn't there, Mrs. Ambrose insisted on reading the Bible with her every day, always focusing on verses about healing and God's will. She turned the envelope over in her hand. The smart thing was to not even open it. But what if Pres wanted to tell her something important? After all, they'd been friends for many more years than they were sweethearts. "No. I'll read it, and then it will have to be destroyed to kill the germs."

Mrs. Ambrose changed the bed, then helped Maureen with a sponge bath before she donned a clean night gown. Afterward, Maureen snuggled into her clean bed, exhausted. How could the simple task of bathing and changing clothes make her feel as if she'd ridden her bicycle clear around the lake, taking the hills at full speed? She'd been looking forward to reading Preston's letter, but right now all she wanted to do was take a nap.

A knock on the door sounded and she opened her eyes. "Come in." Instead of Mrs. Ambrose, Doctor Murphy stepped in. A medical mask covered his face. "I understand your fever finally broke. That's wonderful news." He came a bit closer and pulled a chair up several feet from the bed. In addition to the mask, he'd started wearing gloves he said a doctor on the east coast had recently developed for protection against infection. He pulled out a notepad and pencil and jotted some notes.

Although she enjoyed the company of Mrs. Ambrose, she especially enjoyed her time with Doctor Murphy. And it was easy to understand how Mama thought the doctor would make a good match for her. The gentleness in his voice and the way they chatted more like friends rather than patient and doctor made her feel at peace and cared for. He'd be an easy man to fall for, but she wasn't yet ready to put Preston behind her. She'd read his letter after the doctor left and probably cry herself back to sleep.

Doctor Murphy returned the pad and pencil to his case and the lines around his eyes creased, indicating a smile had emerged beneath the mask. "The first good bit of information I was able to note about you. It was touch and go there for a while."

She frowned. "Was I that bad? You never told me."

"I didn't want to say anything because a patient needs encouragement. But there were a few days when we were afraid you wouldn't make it."

A vague memory drifted through her thoughts of feeling like her whole body was on fire and Mrs. Ambrose tending her with wet compresses on her head and wiping down her entire body while uttering prayers. "I'm afraid I cost Mrs. Ambrose a great deal of lost sleep."

"Better for your nurse to lose sleep than for your family to lose you. It wasn't only your nurse who lost sleep but them as well. Lots of prayers were said those days and nights, by all of us."

Maureen blinked. "I had no idea."

"I know." He moved to stand. "One more week, and I should be able to release you from quarantine."

"Released from jail you mean."

He settled back in the chair. "I'm sure it sometimes feels that way."

Her thoughts went to what Da had told her about Preston being arrested and put in jail for a night. How awful it must have been to wake up in such a place.

She stirred and tried to raise herself onto her elbow. "I'm sure this is nothing like real jail. Thanks for all you and Mrs. Ambrose have done."

"Most of the credit goes to your nurse. I'm only the encourager. I'll be back next week to check on you, and hopefully lift the quarantine."

The door shut quietly behind him as he left, and she reached for the letter. The time had come to see what Preston had to say —good or bad.

CHAPTER FOURTEEN

*P*reston halted his horse, Dusty, outside of William Napper's boat shop and stared out at Geneva Lake, taking in the early morning calm of the blue water. The morning sun reflected off the hints of fall colors among the leaves not yet turned, giving the illusion of a watercolor painting.

He'd heard Napper was looking for a man to help build steam yachts. He knew boats as well as any man and loved them —or did.

The boats were mostly constructed indoors until time to test sea-worthiness come spring. Would he be ready by then to be on water again? Just the thought made him feel like someone was using an egg beater in his stomach. He had half a mind to turn the horse around and head home.

The only other job opening he'd heard of was for a night watchman position for Geneva Cruises who ran a fleet of steam yachts for sightseeing excursions and transportation. But it was short-term since the boats were due to be put up for winter storage soon.

He looked over at Napper's building, then down shore

toward the city docks where Geneva Cruises headquartered. Maybe he'd check on the night watchman job and take his chances another opportunity would come up at Napper's when he was feeling better.

MAUREEN RAN her finger under the envelope and broke the wax seal. She slid out the single sheet of paper and smiled at Preston's familiar scrawl. The handwriting was cramped, no doubt to make all he had to say fit on the small notecard.

My dearest Mo,

I heard you've come down with smallpox. I'm praying you're staying strong and fighting the infection with your usual spunk.

I regret a thousand times over how harsh I was the night I broke things off, then later, couldn't bring myself to tell you during our train ride the next morning what happened after we'd parted.

Maybe you caught smallpox when that baby sneezed on you. I wish I'd never suggested going to the fair. I'm so sorry!

I'm still having nightmares and hate that I have such an unfounded fear of being on water. Why is God punishing me?

I've come to the conclusion it's best if we don't see each other at all. Even as friends. You deserve better. I'm praying for your healing, and hope you're able to live the life God intends for you.

Pres

She swallowed against the walnut-sized lump in her throat and tried in vain to blink away her tears. It was time to admit to herself that since returning to Lake Geneva she'd come to realize how she and Pres weren't as good of a match as she'd thought. They both needed someone to temper their adventurous spirits, not encourage them to points beyond acceptability.

She returned the note to the envelope and left it on the nightstand for Mrs. Ambrose to burn. Best it not be kept for rereading because the quicker she could forget their brief time as sweethearts the better. If Pinkertons didn't work out, she'd find something else to do with her life. Maybe she could become a caretaker like Mrs. Ambrose. Helping others get through this infernal disease. She'd ask Doctor Murphy about it when he came next.

PRESTON NUDGED DUSTY, with his heels to get him moving toward the city docks. If only he could return to when he first left for collage and start over. Not by going to Yale, but by standing up to Dad and making him realize he was no more cut out to sit at a desk than his brothers were to build boats for a living. Life around boats and on water was what he'd always wanted, and college would not help him develop the skills he needed.

He glanced out at Geneva Lake. No sane person could be filled with paralyzing fear at the sight of such calm waters. But he was.

Near the docks, he halted Dusty and stared at the sky. White cumulous clouds floated overhead. Even they sent a chill down his spine. Clouds brought storms and storms caused boats to capsize and … people to die. "What am I supposed to do, God? Why do you let these demons torment me?"

He waited through silence. God wasn't handing out answers, but he wasn't giving up. He'd get the night watchman job, and when he felt more at ease being close to the water, he'd take the next step—whatever that was.

At the docks, he hitched the horse to a post and walked

across the pier, keeping his focus on a man wearing a rumpled white hat who stood next to the only steamboat tied to the dock. He didn't dare look at the water.

The man lifted his head as Preston approached. The unique cut of his beard—angled sideways to each side so his cigar ashes wouldn't burn it—told Preston it was William Napper. The very man he'd just tried to avoid.

Preston held out his hand. "Good morning. I'm looking for the man in charge of Geneva Lake Cruises. Do you know where I might find him?"

Napper shook his head. "He left about an hour or so ago. I expect he'll be back soon. Something I can help you with?"

Preston stared at his feet, keeping his focus there and not on the water lapping against the dock's posts just inches away. "I heard there was an opening for a night watchman and wanted to apply. Do you know if it's still open?"

The man nodded. "I think so. You're welcome to stick around. Wes should be back soon." He narrowed his eyes. "Don't mean to be nosy but you look too well-bred for a position like that."

A sinking feeling washed over Preston. Maybe he should have worn the dungarees he'd worn at the lifesaving station. "I've always made a practice of looking my best when applying for a position, no matter the job. I really do need work. Earning a salary with night hours, frees me up for what needs doing during the day."

The man nodded. "Sounds reasonable to me. He stuck out his hand. "Name's William Napper, but most everyone calls me Mate. I build boats at the west end of the bay."

It would be easy to ask him about the job in his boat shop. But since he didn't mention it, maybe it was filled already. He shook his hand. "Preston Stevens. Pleased to meet you. I'll be on my way so you can get to your work. Hopefully by the time you see me I'll have work of my own."

Mate frowned. "Are you Horace Stevens' boy? We built a steam yacht for him a few years ago. The *Ida*."

Why did he have to give his last name? "Yes, he's my father. I'm taking a break from college and am watching over the lake house this coming winter. Dad will be up in a few weeks to put the *Ida* in drydock. I'll tell him we met. Have a good day." He turned on his heel and left before Mate could ask any more questions. He hadn't lied. Everything he said was true. Sort of.

Dusty whinnied and bobbed his head as Preston approached. He rubbed the star-shaped white spot under the horse's forelock. "I suppose you're looking for a snack." He reached in his back pocket for one of the two carrots he'd brought with him.

While Dusty enjoyed his treat, Preston remounted and stared off at the lake, relieved that through the conversation with Mate he was able to keep his fear in check by focusing on Mate's face. He had to get the watchman job. Slowly acclimating himself to being near the water during a time when there was little activity had to be the way to overcome this thing. After all, nothing noteworthy or dangerous happened this far north of the city.

A couple of hours later, Preston returned to the docks, wearing dungarees and a work shirt. He found the man he presumed to be Wes Johnson on the deck of the *Majestic* checking the engine. "Mr. Johnson?" The man turned. "That would be me. What can I do for you?"

Preston introduced himself and the man lifted his hat from his head revealing his thick dark hair sprinkled with gray. "Mate called a short while ago and said you might be stopping by about the watchman job. Come aboard and let's talk." He walked over to a pair of chairs set up for passengers and sat in one.

Preston pushed down the familiar fear and hopped aboard. "Thank you, sir." He settled in the chair Mr. Johnson had indicated.

Over the next several minutes he answered Johnson's questions as honestly as he could, thankful that he'd been able to keep his emotions in check.

"I like what I'm hearing," Mr. Johnson said. "And I like that you are interested in boating and are native to the area. I'm hoping to add a double-decker to the fleet by next year. If things work out, maybe you'd be interested in applying for the crew."

Preston couldn't help but smile. If that worked out, it would add to the needed experience to acquire his own fleet someday. "That sounds wonderful, Mr. Johnson. I'd definitely be interested in that opportunity."

"Good. When can you start on the watchman job?"

"As soon as you want me."

"Be here tomorrow night at eight. You'll work until six the next morning. I know it's a long stint, but it means a larger paycheck than an eight-hour day. And one more thing. We're informal around here. Everyone calls me Wes." He stood and held out his hand.

Preston shook his hand. "Thanks, Wes. Will I see you tomorrow night when I report?"

"No. Stan Harris will be here. He works from noon until eight. He'll stay a little longer tomorrow night to help you acclimate."

A short time later, Preston stopped in Sculley's Mercantile on Main Street and bought several pairs of work dungarees and a couple of long-sleeved shirts, determined to not fail at this job. It was his last hope.

CHAPTER FIFTEEN

Maureen looked up as her mother stepped into the room, a face mask covering her beautiful features. "Mama, what are you doing here? Is Mrs. Ambrose okay?"

"She's washing your linens. Your scabs are coming off now, and she said as long as I wear a mask I shouldn't worry. Dr. Murphy is here to check on you. I told him you are feeling much better. Is it okay to let him in, or do you need to do anything first?"

"What would I have to do before he comes in?"

"I was thinking maybe run a brush through your hair. The fever has brought out the natural curls you inherited from your granny. They are beautiful, but not when you've been lying on them for days. Why did you take the braid out?"

Her mother still persisted in her matchmaking despite Maureen's illness. As nice and handsome as the doctor was, she doubted he had any interest in a woman with scars. Besides, as soon as she was well, she intended on moving to the city. "Mrs. Ambrose always makes the plaits too tight. The braid pulled at my scalp. Dr. Murphy has seen me at my worst. What does it matter?"

Mama shrugged. "Just thinking ahead to when you are better."

Maureen skimmed her right cheek with her fingertips and her chest tightened. The scarring felt worse than it did yesterday. What had she done so terrible that God had to punish her this way? "You can stop getting ideas about the doctor and me being a good match. With this face, no man would want me."

Her mother winced. "When a good man sees your heart, he will forget about the face." She turned toward the door. "I'll tell the doctor to come in."

The door clicked behind her, and Maureen shifted her back against the pillows. At the fair, she'd watched as Preston turned his head whenever a beautiful woman passed by. Beauty attracted and ugly scars repelled. In that area, Preston was like every man. She still planned to apply at Pinkertons, and if they weren't interested, she'd volunteer at the smallpox infirmaries set up in the city. No one was allowed in those wretched centers unless they were immune. It was probably the only place she'd ever feel comfortable again.

The door opened and Doctor Murphy stepped in, the ever-present face mask covering everything but those intense blue eyes that rivaled Geneva Lake on a clear summer day. She enjoyed seeing them almost as much as viewing the lake.

He pulled a straight-backed chair over and sat next to the bed. "Good morning, Maureen."

She managed a smile. "Since I'm well enough that my mother can be with me as long as she wears a mask, does that mean I'm not contagious?"

"The lines around his eyes deepened. Mrs. Ambrose did a full inspection when she bathed you earlier and said your few remaining scabs look like they're ready to fall off. I'm ready to declare you noncontagious. And since that's the case ... he reached behind his head and loosened the ties, then pulled the mask away from his face. "There is no need for my wearing this."

She couldn't help staring at his beard, neatly trimmed, which was her preference. The thick bushy ones some men favored made them appear rough around the edges. "I'd forgotten you have a beard."

He threw his head back and laughed. "You don't remember saying I looked like your father when he was my age?"

She loved the way Da laughed in much the same way. Had some of the rock-hard resistance to Mama's suggestion about Doctor Murphy chipped away? She could do worse, and if anything, she needed a friend since Preston had ended that relationship as well. "Yes. Now I remember. I think the fever affected my memory."

He stared at her a moment too long and she cast about for something to say. Anything to get this conversation back to patient and doctor. "Does this mean I can return to the house and my sister can have the cottage back for all of her last days as a single woman?"

He held up a hand, palm out. "Not so fast. You are going to be too weak to climb stairs for the next several days. Let's see how you are by the weekend. You can help by doing a few muscle exercises that Mrs. Ambrose will show you. Today is Monday. Let's make Saturday your goal for moving to the house."

"I can live with that." She pushed herself to a sitting position. "Can you please hand me that hand mirror on the dresser."

He turned and retrieved the mirror. "I will give this to you, but you must prepare yourself before you look. Remember that the scabs just came off and the scars are quite prominent. Just like the scars you probably received from scraping your knee when you were small, time will cause them to fade."

She winced. "In other words, they'll still be there."

"Yes. Perhaps you'd like Mrs. Ambrose and your mother to be here when you look at the mirror."

She barely heard his comment, spoken so softly. "Yes. That would be nice."

The doctor stood and stepped to the door, then opened it a few inches. "Mrs. Ambrose and Mrs. Quinn, Maureen would like you both here. She's going to look at herself in the mirror."

A few moments later, the older women stepped inside. Mama didn't wear a mask, but stood just inside the door while Mrs. Ambrose, her gray eyes full of concern, came to the bed and sat on its side. She took Maureen's hand and squeezed it. "Are you sure you want to do this now? Perhaps a few more days—"

"I don't want to wait. I need to see for myself what I'm dealing with." Maureen searched the woman's face with her eyes. The first couple of days Mrs. Ambrose had taken care of her, the scars on the woman's face were all she saw. But nowadays she hardly noticed. Would that be the same for her family? For her friends? "Please?"

"All right. Go ahead and hand her the mirror, Doctor."

Maureen took the mirror Doctor Murphy held out and laid it face down on her chest. She closed her eyes. *Lord please give me strength for this moment.*

She lifted the mirror, turned it toward herself, and opened her eyes.

Burning bile rose to her throat and her stomach heaved. She swallowed hard and flung the mirror against the wall. It dropped to the floor, the sound of shattering glass assuring she'd never have to see herself in it again. Her stomach heaved once more, and she pressed a fist to her mouth. She faced the wall. "Perhaps it would be better if I never leave the house again."

Mrs. Ambrose gently touched her shoulder. "It's a shock

now, Maureen, but in time it will get easier. She stood. "I want to show you something. I have to leave but will be right back."

The door clicked shut and Maureen turned over. Her mother's sad expression was as she expected it to be. But Dr. Murphy's was not. Instead, he regarded her with the same kind expression he had when he handed her the mirror.

She focused on the ceiling. "You don't have to pretend you don't see my ugliness, Doctor. I'm a big girl."

"I don't see ugliness, Maureen. I see the same fun-loving beautiful girl you've always been."

She snapped her focus back to him. "Fun? This isn't fun. My sister is going to marry in a couple of weeks, and I'm to be her maid of honor. I can't do that with this face."

"Of course, you can."

The door opened and Mrs. Ambrose retook her seat next to Maureen. She held out a hand mirror. "I fetched this from one of the bedrooms, but I'll be holding it instead of you. Just in case."

Maureen hadn't missed the twinkle in the woman's eye. How could she not go along with this woman's sweet spirit? "Okay,"

"Before you look, turn your head to the left." She held up the mirror to Maureen's right.

Maureen did as directed and glanced toward the mirror, seeing smooth skin from her forehead to her chin, without scabs or pocks. She then turned her head and viewed the left side of her face, scarred and ugly.

One side normal in appearance and the other pocked. They'd talked before about how she only had scabs on the left side of her face. How had she forgotten that now? "How did that happen?"

"I have no idea, "Doctor Murphy said. "Sometimes the spots appear in strange patterns, but I've never seen it done quite this way."

Maureen sighed. "I can't go through life only showing my right side to people. I'm still doomed."

"Nonsense." Mrs. Ambrose handed the mirror to the doctor and he placed it on the dresser.

"I've learned to live with the scars and you will too." The older woman patted her shoulder. "I like to call them my battle wounds. We who have survived smallpox have been through a war. The disease tried to kill us or at least render us unuseful, but God doesn't let our trials be wasted one bit. He uses them to His glory, and you are not excluded from that privilege."

Maureen curled into a fetal position. If God loved her like the Bible says, why did he let this happen? Maybe tomorrow she'd feel the same as Mrs. Ambrose, but not today. Right now, all she wanted was to sleep. At least when asleep she didn't have to lie there and feel sorry for herself.

Five Days Later

MAUREEN STEPPED through the cottage's open door and lifted her face to the warm early October sun that offset the morning chill. She glanced around at the trees towering overhead, all wearing spots of gold and red against the dark green leaves that were trying so hard to hang on to summer. Had so much time gone by since she was placed on quarantine? "It must be a good sign that my first day among the living is such a beautiful one."

"So it is my bonnie lass." Da grinned then picked up Mrs. Ambrose's satchel and carried it toward the waiting phaeton. She insisted Da use it to take Mrs. Ambrose home instead of his preferred wagon. Knowing Mrs. Ambrose, Maureen was sure the woman would never complain about her mode of transportation, but Mama was right. The phaeton's upholstered seat was far more comfortable for the hour's ride than the wagon's hard bench.

Maureen drew the older woman into a hug "Words can't express my gratitude for the care you gave me. Without it I doubt I would have survived."

"With God's help and your grit and determination I'm sure you would have, but it's better when one is so ill that there is someone standing by to assist. Hopefully one day smallpox will be removed forever."

Mama stepped closer. "I'm mounting a campaign to get everyone I know to take the vaccination. I never did, and it never occurred to me to have my children vaccinated until this happened."

Mrs. Ambrose nodded. "You aren't the only ones who didn't take advantage of the vaccine. Look at all those who have come down with it in Chicago. I've heard it won't be long before vaccinations will be required for all school children. I've just been notified of a woman in Elkhorn who has it now, and it's believed she picked up the virus at the World's Fair. Stands to reason with all those people attending from all over the world."

"I'm almost certain that's where I caught it," Maureen said. "I plan to go into Chicago as soon as I get my strength back to tend to some things. I wish there was a way to track down the mother of that baby who sneezed on me while I was there. I'd like to know if he came down with it."

Mama stared at Maureen. "You may learn more than you want. If he had small pox, he may not have survived. I can't believe you want to go to the city after all you've been through. Whatever for?"

She may as well tell them now. "To apply for a job at the Pinkerton Agency. If they won't take me as an apprentice agent, I might apply to work in the office. Let them get to know me and maybe they'll move me up to apprenticing as a detective."

Concern filled Da's eyes. "Where would you live?"

She needed an answer fast. Saying she hadn't thought that far would not go over well. "I'm hoping Sophie will let me stay at her house, or else I can inquire at the church that sponsored the mission school Mama taught at before the fire. Wasn't it called Illinois Street Church?"

Her mother's face softened. "Yes, it was, but it's no longer on Illinois Street. They renamed it the Chicago Avenue church since that's where they rebuilt. I don't suppose anything I say will dissuade you from your plans. Check with them for suggestions on a place to stay if you can't be at Sophie's. At least if you're at one of those places, I won't worry so much."

The family walked Mrs. Ambrose to the waiting carriage. Da helped her onto the seat then circled around the phaeton and climbed in. He clicked his tongue and the horse started toward the front gate. Mrs. Ambrose stuck her head out from beneath the carriage's canopy and waved.

Maureen didn't move until Da turned onto Snake Road and moved out of sight. She faced her mother. "I'd like to walk down to the shore for a few minutes before I come inside. It's been a long while since I've been near the water.

"All right but don't overdo. We want you rested by the wedding on Saturday. You have to be ready to be the maid of honor."

Her heart fell. "I told Katie to let Mary Lou have the job."

"She told me. But Katie really wants you. I told her to leave it as is. Besides, the dress is fitted for you and no one else."

Maureen pressed her lips together then let out the breath she was holding. "It's likely too big for me now. I've lost weight since I was last fitted."

"That's why Millie is sending her assistant, Trudy, out this afternoon to retake your measurements. Millie is getting up in years, and it's difficult for her to get down on her knees anymore. We're hoping Trudy can make the adjustments while she is here."

Maureen set her jaw and turned away. "I can't be in the wedding, Mama."

"Look at me and tell me why. You were so excited when Katie asked you to be her maid of honor."

She whipped around and positioned herself so the left side of her face was in full view. "Look at this. A wedding is supposed to be beautiful. Not only the bride, but the wedding party, the setting, all of it. Katie is only saying she still wants me out of kindness. I intend to remain on the veranda in the shadows and watch from there, out of sight."

Mama's eyes filled and she blinked. "You're exaggerating. Yes, you are scarred, but it's not as bad as you think."

"You don't understand. How can I expect you to when all your life you've been beautiful?"

Her mother's arms came around her from behind. "I can't begin to understand, but if you think I look the same as I did at your age, you're wrong. I have wrinkles now and lines, my hair is starting to gray. Beauty doesn't last forever for any of us. For your information, I don't even see your scars when I look at you my darling daughter, and I'm sure once people get past their first sight of the new you, they won't notice them either. Not with your spirited personality and kind heart."

She wriggled free of her mother's embrace. "You're biased because you're my mother. I'm going by the lake to think and pray. I'll be in shortly."

As she walked across the lawn the fallen leaves crunched beneath her feet. She bent and picked up a bright orange maple leaf, already its edges browned. Soon the whole leaf would lose its attractiveness. Exactly how she felt. A part of her still displayed youthful beauty while another part was marred forever. Much like the rest of her body that only she saw when she bathed. Any husband would be repulsed by the scars that covered every part of her. Could a Protestant become a nun? A nun's habit would suit her fine. At least then Mama would stop trying to be a matchmaker.

She reached the water and watched the gentle waves lap up against the rocky shoreline. She loved the lake so much. Maybe she should forget applying at Pinkertons and stay right here. She hated how one minute she was determined to go to Chicago and make a life for herself there and the next she wanted to be a recluse and live at Safe Refuge forever. The name of the family home certainly applied to her circumstance.

A few minutes later she returned to the house and stepped inside.

"There you are." Mama stepped out of the kitchen and into the main hall. "Millie's rang a few minutes ago and said Trudy will be here within the hour. I'm preparing some tuna sandwiches for a light lunch. It will only be you and me since your Da won't be back until later, and Richard and Doreen are at school. Perhaps while Trudy is here we can order a couple of new dresses for you."

"That won't be necessary."

Her mother quirked her head. "I thought some new clothes would please you after such a terrible bout of illness. Nothing like a new gown or two to make a woman feel pretty."

"I've decided to become a nun."

CHAPTER SIXTEEN

*N*ate approached the Quinn's main house and pulled the bell next to the door. It felt strange and good at the same time that he was coming to see Maureen in the family home instead of quarantined to the cottage.

Mrs. Quinn opened the door. "Hello Doctor Murphy." She stepped aside to allow him to enter. Maureen is on the veranda."

"How has she been doing since the quarantine was lifted?"

"At first, she declared she'd decided to become a nun so she could live in a cloister and never venture out in public but hasn't mentioned it lately. Other than that, I suppose she's doing all right considering what she's been through. She's still struggling quite a bit and has only gone outside after dark to walk to the lakeshore. She doesn't think she can be the maid of honor in Katie's wedding next week because of her scars. Maybe you can convince her it's not as bad as she thinks."

He shook his head. "I can try, but I fear too much cajoling might lead to her digging in her heels."

"I know what you mean." Mrs. Quinn led the way through the home's center hall and out to the veranda. "Maureen, someone is here to see you."

"I don't want to see anyone. I told you that before."

"Dr. Murphy has already seen your face and he needs to check on your progress. I won't turn him away." She beckoned Nate to come outside.

"Okay, but I don't know why he'd bother. Nothing has changed since he released me from quarantine."

He stepped onto the veranda and stood beside Mrs. Quinn. At the sight of Maureen, his heart raced. Only the unmarred side of her face was in view. But he found either side equally attractive. Would he ever convince her of that? "You may be out of quarantine, but you can't get rid of me that fast."

Mrs. Quinn stepped toward the door. "She's all yours, Doctor. I hope you can convince her that she can't be a recluse. I'll go back to what I was doing."

After Mrs. Quinn left, Maureen glanced up at Nate, her green eyes intense. "I suppose you're here to tell me to start living again by agreeing to be in Katie's wedding."

He stepped closer and had to work to not stare. She was stunning, even with scars covering half her face. Snapping out of his thoughts, he dragged a chair next to her and sat. "I'm not here to tell you anything. You will join the rest of the world when you're ready. But I hope if you sit out the wedding, you won't come to regret it later."

Tears appeared in the corners of her eyes. "I'll face that when the time comes."

"Why don't you ask your sister how she feels about it? It must mean a lot to her for you to be a part of the ceremony."

"She asked me before I got sick. I might be doing her a favor by backing out. In fact, I may not attend the wedding at all. I can watch unnoticed from here on the veranda."

"Your sister—"

"We may share the same last name, but she's really my cousin. Maybe you didn't know."

He worked to say his next words as gentle as possible. "I

have been told she is your father's niece, but she was officially adopted by your parents after she was orphaned. That makes her your sister."

She bit her trembling lower lip and turned her head. "I know. We truly are sisters and have been since before I was born. I don't know why I said that, but she still can't want me in her wedding. I look like a freak."

"I doubt she sees you that way. Nor do your parents. Or I, for that matter."

She faced him, her tear-filled eyes wide. "How can you not see the pocks?"

"Because I see beyond the skin and into your heart. We've had a lot of talks over the past weeks. I've admired your concern for everyone around you. Mrs. Ambrose because she never took a day off. Your parents because they were worried sick about you and unable to be with you. And your friends that they didn't catch smallpox after being with you." He paused a moment. "Even me. You were concerned for all the time I spent with you, and even though I told you the mask was precautionary because although I have been vaccinated we don't know how long the vaccine will work. Why this shift in attitude from others to yourself?"

She shrugged, a motion of indifference, but he knew she was struggling. "I thought the scarring wouldn't be this bad. I've seen the looks of disgust on the few people who have seen me since I came out of quarantine. They remember me as I was before, and now they see this." She waved her hand over the left side of her face. "It's going to be like that through the wedding and reception. Maybe if I stay here on the veranda and sit in the shadows, I can be there without being there."

Nate doubted the expressions she saw were made intentionally to hurt her. People needed to be warned before they saw her for the first time, but how? "Perhaps when you stand next to

Katie during the ceremony you can stand with the right side of your face toward the people."

"I still have to walk up and down the aisle. By the end of the wedding everyone will see my awful side." She looked off at the lake then faced him. "I've been thinking of joining a convent."

He decided it best not to mention her mother had told him about her idea. "I didn't realize your family was Catholic."

"We're not. I plan to find out if converts can become nuns. I know it's vain, but a nun's habit covers a good part of the side of the face. And don't they mostly spend their time in seclusion, away from people?"

He shrugged. "I saw my share of nuns out and about when I lived in Columbus. They're not always secluded. Many teach school or work as nurses. Regardless, is that a good reason to become a nun?"

She shook her head. "Not really." She faced him. ". But I don't think I can handle people's stares and looks of disgust."It was only a thought. Last night, I threw out the idea to my parents and Da about had a fit. How was I to know that's the church his family attended before he left to join a different one, causing his da to disown him?"

Now some of the pieces were coming together. "And then his family died in the great fire."

"Yes. Da went to their apartment the day of the fire to try to reconcile, but his da wouldn't let him in. He never had a chance to talk to them or the rest of the family again. Katie was with neighbors and they brought her to safety and eventually to Irish Woods. I'll save the rest of the story for another time."

"I look forward to hearing it."

"It may be a while. I've decided to move to the city as soon as I'm stronger. New people don't have my old face to compare to. In the city I can fade into the crowd." She sighed. "I still don't feel comfortable being in the wedding but will lean on the Lord and He'll get me through it. I won't let Katie down."

He grinned. "He promises to never leave us or forsake us. And I'm sure he'll give you whatever you need to get through the day."

She took a small note card from her skirt pocket. "Mrs. Ambrose gave me this verse from Proverbs before she moved home and advised me to read it often." She read it aloud, "Favor is deceitful, and beauty is vain: but a woman that feareth the LORD, she shall be praised."

He couldn't stop himself from smiling. "That's the perfect verse for you, Maureen."

"I'm sure it is, but I'm not there yet. I was very angry with God when I was burning with fever and covered with sores. A lot of that anger has changed to acceptance but there is still some there."

"Sometimes we need to give ourselves permission to be mad at God. He's bigger than all our anger. How is your energy level?"

She shrugged. "I tire easily."

"I have a cure for that." He stood and held out his hand. "Come on. Stand up."

She stared at his open palm. "Why?"

"We're going for a walk. A little exercise is good for the body, and it will help your stamina. Get you strong enough to ride that bicycle of yours again."

She looked up at him, her luminous green eyes almost taking his breath away. "How far will we go?"

"When you begin to tire we'll turn around."

"Okay. As long as we walk away from town and not toward it."

"Where we might run into people who knew you before." He said it as a statement and not a question.

She offered him a tentative smile. "Right."

"Then, let's go." Before she could change her mind, he took her hand and drew her to a standing position then led her to the steps leading to the lawn below. Her hand seemed to fit in his so perfectly, and he decided to continue to hold it as she made her way down the several steps to the grass. If she didn't want to hold hands, she'd let him know.

They stepped onto the grass, and she tugged her hand free. There was his answer. The line between patient and physician was becoming more and more blurred. He had to be careful. He offered her his elbow and she slipped her hand around his upper arm. They started down the slope to the path, her gait quite uneven. He stopped. "Are you okay? You seem to be a little unsteady."

Her face turned an adorable shade of pink. "I was hoping you hadn't noticed. I wanted to wear something fun today and decided to wear my party shoes instead of my usual boots. The small heel sinks into the ground so I'm walking on my toes."

"Do you want to turn around?"

"She shook her head. "We're almost to the path where the ground is harder. I'll be fine."

"I could go back and get your boots."

"I'm sure we won't go far. It's okay."

He slowed his pace, despite her assurances. They reached the well-worn path and he caught a good look at her shoes, expensive looking. The ground may be firm, but it was still dirt. He should have gone back for her boots.

They headed west. He'd insist they turn back if they made it as far as Blackloft, the modest two-story home that sat high on a hill several properties down. "What was it like growing up on such a beautiful lake, Maureen?" He surveyed the calm water, as blue as the sky. "I imagine your childhood here must have been almost magical."

"We're not like most of the lakeshore people. I attended the public school in town and had chores. Mama grew up very wealthy. She had maids, cooks, and drivers who took them everywhere in their carriages. She decided her children would learn from a young age how to do for themselves. Da immigrated from Ireland with his parents. They barely made ends meet. I guess you can say the Quinns are a blend of both worlds."

"Coming from two different backgrounds, how did your parents meet?"

"He was a janitor at a mission school, and she was a teacher there. They fell madly in love and the rest is history, as the saying goes. My granddaddy built the big house, and we lived in the cottage until both my grandparents passed away. Here I've gone on and on about me. What about you? I know you went to medical college in Columbus, Ohio. Is that where you grew up?"

He'd purposely not mentioned much about his past, thinking she might be put off. But hearing what she'd shared, he doubted she'd blink. "My father died when I was a baby and my mother was left to raise me on her own. She went from one housekeeping job to another until I was school age when she found a position as a governess for a wealthy family's two sons.

"Living in a small apartment in their house was the first stability I'd known. We lived there until I was in high school and the boys didn't need a governess anymore. By then I could work after school, and Mother went back to housekeeping jobs. I moved to Columbus and worked my way through medical college." He stopped walking. "We're already to Blackloft. Perhaps we should—"

Maureen wobbled and fell forward. "Oh!"

He reached for her arm and missed. She crumbled to the ground.

His pulse racing, he knelt beside her, relieved she was alert and attempting to sit up. "Maureen, don't move until I check to make sure you're okay."

She nodded and pressed her lips together as though trying to keep her pain hidden. He pressed two fingers to her wrist. The pulse was good.

"I think I twisted my foot."

"We'd better check it. Feeling awkward, he gently lifted her skirt to expose her ankle. Why was she wearing those gaiters? Was she planning to take a bicycle ride. Knowing her it wouldn't surprise him."

He slid the shoe off, then glanced around the grass until he spotted what he was looking for and picked it up. "The heel came off your shoe. That's why you fell." He chuckled. "And I assume by the gaiters you planned on more than sitting on the veranda today."

She looked down and closed her eyes, her dark eye lashes fanning across her skin. "Guilty as charged. I'm so sick of being inside and inactive. I thought I might give the wheel a try, even if it was only in the circular drive."

Now wasn't the time for lectures although a few words sat on the tip of his tongue. "Understood. He took hold of her foot and pressed his thumb against the instep. She didn't react. He studied it a moment. "There isn't any visible bruising. The foot appears okay. I'll have to move the gaiter up to inspect the ankle. I'll be careful." He loosened the stirrup that held the gaiter in place around her foot, then rolled the fabric high enough to expose her delicate ankle. He gave it a gentle squeeze.

She recoiled. "Oh, that hurt."

"Can you move your foot at all without pain?"

She did as he asked. "Other than a twinge by the ankle, nothing. I guess I'll live."

"Indeed, you will." He rolled the gaiter back in place and slid the stirrup under her bare foot. "Let's see if you can stand." She gripped his offered hand and he pulled her to her feet.

She put weight on her good foot and took a small step, balancing on the ball of her bad foot. "I think I can walk okay."

"It's best to stay off your feet the rest of the day. We want you able to walk down the aisle at the wedding." She took another step and wobbled. "I'll have to move slowly without the shoe."

"Then it looks like I'll have to carry you."

She crossed her arms. "No. I'm too heavy."

"I'm stronger than you might think. Let's give it a try." He slid his right arm around her waist, then placed his left arm under the backs of her legs and lifted her until they were eye to eye. She wrapped her left arm around his neck and the delicious scent of roses wafted into his nose. He'd expected to struggle a bit but she wasn't heavy at all.

He started walking toward Safe Refuge. They'd reached the property next to Maureen's home when a small yacht skimmed through the water off to their right. Maureen turned her face away as though trying to hide. The boat moved on without whomever was onboard not having noticed them. He took another step. "You can look now. The boat is gone."

She leaned her head back and faced the lake. "That was close."

"Who did you think it was?"

"An old friend. He has a boat like that one. But on second thought, I doubt it was him. Doctor Murphy, are you sure I'm not too heavy? Maybe we should stop for a rest."

He moved toward an Oak tree with overhanging branches that offered a secluded spot if one didn't want to be noticed. "Only if you stop calling me Doctor Murphy. I think we've spent enough time together to be on a first-name basis. Since you are no longer my official patient, please call me Nate."

She offered him a slight smile. "I'm okay with that … Nate. You already do call me Maureen."

He neared the tree and glanced toward the water. A sinking feeling came over him and he set her down. "That boat is returning and coming toward us. The man might want to say something. Let's hope he's not your friend. Try not to put weight on the bad ankle."

The boat came close enough to hear the man's shout. "Looks like the lady needs assistance."

Recognizing the voice, Nate stepped closer to the shore. "Good morning, Mate. Out testing one of your new boats?"

"I thought that was you, Murphy. Just had to make a run over to Williams Bay. You need a ride somewhere?"

"Thanks, but we're only going as far as Safe Refuge. Maureen turned her ankle, but she's not any trouble to carry."

Mate offered a knowing smile. "I can see now that's Maureen Quinn with you." He turned his attention to her. "Tell your father I said hello."

She gave him a smile that looked forced. "I will, Mr. Napper."

Mate waved an acknowledgment, then backed the boat away and turned toward the village.

Maureen sighed. "I hope he believes my injury was the only reason you were carrying me."

Nate chuckled. "What do you mean?"

"It's not proper behavior for a woman to be carried like you've been carrying me unless there's a good reason."

He grinned as he bent to lift her. "And your having sprained your ankle isn't a good enough reason? I thought you enjoyed breaking societal rules. But I wouldn't worry about Mate. He's a good man."

He raised Maureen up to eye level and their gazes met. Mesmerized by her eyes that reminded him of emeralds, he didn't move.

She searched his face with her eyes. "And you are a good man, Nate Murphy."

She brought her face closer and the fragrance of roses almost sent him into an intoxicating spell. His gaze moved to her lips, naturally pink and inviting. Before he could stop himself, he brought his mouth to her lips and fell hopelessly lost in the moment. Her clasped hands at the nape of his neck pulled him closer. He took a step farther under the tree, making them invisible to anyone on the water or the path. He ended the kiss to catch his breath than trailed a string of kisses over her face, finally landing on her lips and deepening the kiss.

They parted and he drew her close as she pressed her face against his chest. He had so much to say but the words didn't come.

"Doctor Murphy, if this is your prescription to make me stronger, it's failed miserably. I'm as weak as a new born foal right now." Maureen leaned back and looked him in the eyes. "I had no idea you had kisses like that in your little black bag."

He eased her down to her feet. "You're not the only one feeling weak. I could say the same about your kiss as well." He drew her into a hug. "I've been wanting to do that for a long time."

"How long?"

He chuckled. "Probably since the first time I laid eyes on you in the furniture store. I didn't think you'd think highly of me if I followed my inclination."

"You're probably right, but I have been wondering for quite a few weeks now how your beard would feel if you kissed me." She ran her fingertips along his whiskers. "It's so soft. I didn't even notice it like I thought I would."

He grinned. "Does that mean you want me to kiss you again?"

She giggled. "I wouldn't mind."

His lips found hers and she cupped her hand around his neck. The tiniest of sounds like the mews of a kitten came from her throat and the kiss deepened. Could they stay there the rest of the afternoon? Of course, they couldn't. He ended the kiss then kissed the tip of her nose. "Best we get you home."

"I know. Although I wouldn't mind staying here a bit longer."

"We'll do it again soon." He lifted her up and stepped out from beneath the canopy of leaves.

"Thank you, Nate."

"For what?"

"Kissing my face, both sides, not only the pretty side."

He stopped walking and stared down into her eyes. "There is no good side and bad side. You are a beautiful person inside and out."

She snuggled her head under his chin. "If that's what you see when you look at me, that's all that matters."

At her veranda, he set her in the chair she'd occupied earlier. She arranged her skirt and he noticed a glow about her that hadn't been there before. Was he glowing too? He almost felt like it. If her mother had an inkling of what they were doing a few minutes ago she may not be very happy. "Let's get you comfortable. I still have a couple of house calls to make."

She giggled. "I hope this kind of house call is reserved only for me."

"Well, you won't have to worry about my next one. "Mort Gibson is going to be ninety on his next birthday. He's not my type. As for the second, I doubt Mrs. Deignan's husband would be pleased." He ran his gaze over her face and smoothed a loose curl off her left cheek. "You're the one and only patient I intend to kiss. In case you haven't figured it out, you've become very special to me."

"As you have to me, Nate."

The door to the house opened behind him and he straightened and jumped back.

Mrs. Quinn stepped onto the porch. She gave a curious look. "I saw you carrying Maureen up the hill. What happened?"

"She twisted her ankle. It's not severe, but I carried her to avoid hurting it any worse. She should stay off of it until the wedding. It should be okay by then."

Mrs. Quinn dropped to her knees and stared at Maureen's foot where it rested on the ottoman. "Where is your shoe?"

Nate laughed and produced it from his back pocket. "I

almost forgot. The heel broke off, which is why she fell in the first place." He handed her the shoe and the detached heel.

"How far down the path had you gone?"

"Just to Blackloft." Maureen said. "Nate carried me as though I was as light as a kitten." She smiled at him.

He looked away for fear if they locked gazes again they'd give themselves away.

Mrs. Quinn's left brow rose and she looked at Nate then Maureen. "Seems Maureen lost a heel and the doctor lost his last name."

Maureen laughed. "We decided since I'm no longer an official patient, it was too formal to call him Doctor Murphy."

Mrs. Quinn smiled at Nate. "Well then, if you are off duty, I'll call you Nate as well and ask if you'd like to join the family for dinner. It will be ready in about an hour when Mr. Quinn gets home. Katie and her fiancé will be joining us. You may as well meet the rest of the clan."

Nate's shoulders relaxed. Would Reverend and Mrs. Olsen understand if he bowed out of their dinner invitation? They already knew a medical emergency might happen. Best he stick to his obligations. "It's very kind of you to invite me, I'd love to stay but I already have plans for the evening. Perhaps another time?"

She nodded. "Of course. We'll arrange for a date after the wedding."

"I'm looking forward to it." He faced Maureen. "If you have a supply of ice, wrap some in a towel and hold it on the ankle to help keep the swelling down."

"I will. Promise. I can at least walk you to the door, or maybe I should say hobble you to the door."

"Maureen, the doctor—Nate—said you should stay off your feet. I'll escort him to the door. You'll see him again at the wedding and you can show him how strong you are on your feet by then."

She sank back on her chair and looked at Nate, her face full of disappointment. Was she hoping he'd kiss her again before he left? That would be a perfect end to the afternoon, but probably not wise.

"Just so you know, Mama, I don't intend to stay for the wedding reception. I'm sure being there with Katie during the ceremony will be taxing enough."

Her mother frowned. "Nonsense. Your da can carry you to the tent and I'll provide a chair for you to sit on."

Maureen shrugged. "I'd prefer to sit up here where I am now."

Her mother gaped at her. "You have to attend. The entire family—"

"Will be there along with half the town, all of Irish Woods, and the lake shore people. No thank you."

Her mother let out a sound of exasperation. "Most will have already seen your face during the ceremony. What difference does it make?"

"I don't expect you to understand. I agreed to be in the wedding party, but that's all." She looked up at Nate. "Nate, if you don't mind, can you please help me get upstairs. I've had enough of this day."

CHAPTER SEVENTEEN

*P*reston stepped into Sculley's Mercantile and spotted Mate at the back of the store sifting through a bin of screws. Before he could duck out of sight, Mate saw him and approached. "We met a few weeks ago, didn't we?"

Preston nodded and forced a smile. "Yes. When I was looking for Wes Johnson to apply for the watchman job. I've been there a couple of weeks now."

The older man nodded. "Good to hear." He turned to walk away then faced Preston. "Probably not my business, haven't I seen you in the company of Rory Quinn's daughter a number of times?"

The question caught him off guard, and he worked to gather himself. "Yes. Our families have been friendly for years."

"When I was coming back from Williams Bay a couple of days ago, I saw Maureen walking on the shore path. I'd heard she had smallpox, and it was good to see her looking well."

Preston perked up. "Oh, I hadn't heard she was out of danger. That's wonderful news. I'm surprised she'd be out walking alone so soon."

"She wasn't alone. Nate Murphy, the new doctor was with her."

"Good to hear he was keeping a watchful eye on his patient."

"If that's what you want to call it." He winked and walked off.

Preston's stomach burned hot. Thankful for his new beard that shielded his flaming face, he began looking for what he came into the store for, if only he could remember what it was.

Napper's words continued to grate at him long after he gave up on shopping and stepped out on Main Street. What had Napper seen? Were Maureen and the doctor walking hand in hand? Arm in arm? He pushed the thought of them kissing out of his mind.

She was a girl who liked to take risks, but would she go so far as to kiss a man right there on the shore path? Of course, she would. She returned his own kiss in the middle of the train depot. He wanted to go over to the doctor's office and introduce Murphy to his left hook.

He snapped out of his thoughts. He had no right to feel that way. He broke up with her and she had the right to be with whomever she wanted. Good for her if she and the doctor were seeing each other. What he needed, was to go home and rest up before his shift at the docks tonight.

Instead of turning up Broad Street to get Dusty from the livery, he continued down Main Street and made a turn toward the lake at the boat shop's driveway. The thought crossed his mind to track Napper down and ask what he meant, but he thought better of it. Best to not draw attention to himself. He headed down the shore path, pleased he was able to walk so close to the water. A month earlier he couldn't have done it. He paused his step and glanced around. It had to be around here that Mate saw Maureen and the doc. He continued walking.

The sound of voices broke into his reverie, and he came to a stop. He was at the Quinn property already? He glanced up the hill. Several men, including Rory Quinn and Nate Murphy, were setting out chairs directly in front of the veranda, no doubt for Katie's wedding tomorrow. Off to the right, a large white tent took up almost half of the lawn.

His parents were arriving later today to attend the wedding, and he'd also been invited. He'd never intended to go, but now he wished he hadn't declined. He supposed Nate Murphy would be there too if he was helping to set up. Anger rose into his throat. He turned and marched back toward town. He had to get out of there before one of his migraines took over. The only thing that that seemed to stop one from coming on was a nip and a nap.

PRESTON WOKE TO HIS PARENTS' voices from downstairs drifting into his bedroom. He stretched grateful the headache was gone. Now, to get through the usual interrogation. At least this time he could talk about his new job and how it was going. He dressed in clean dungarees and a work shirt and went downstairs.

On the veranda, His father looked up from the local paper when Preston stepped through the door. "Good afternoon, son. How was your sleep?"

He settled in a chair across from Dad. "Fine. Did you have a good train ride up here?"

Dad folded the newspaper and set it on a rattan side table. "Yes, we did. You've not said anything recently about how you are feeling lately."

"I know. I'm feeling a bit better. I'm still having those nightmares and flashes of anger, but I seem to have it more under control. This morning, something was said to me about Maureen that set me off. I was able to hold it in until I was alone and let off steam then. Still have one of those nasty headaches, but at least I kept everything else in check."

"I hope that goes away soon. You've never had such a temper before, nor migraines. Your mother spoke with Anna Quinn yesterday. Maureen is recovering nicely. Unfortunately, she has some scarring on part of her face, but she is a fortunate young lady."

A vision of Mo and the doctor walking arm in arm down the shore path came into Preston's head and he forced it away. "That's good news."

"Then I take it you haven't communicated with Maureen since the episode in Chicago."

"No. Except for a letter I wrote her while she was quarantined. Never heard back. Just as well since I can't be with anyone until I get past this craziness."

"I understand there's a new doctor in town. Doctor Nathan Murphy is the name I was given. Why don't you make an appointment with him? Tell him what happened during that storm. Maybe his being fresh out of medical training, he'd know more how to treat that kind of thing than an older man."

Preston's stomach heated. "I'm not interested in doing that."

Dad frowned. "You don't have to get snippy about it. Don't you want to get well? Be able to do what you've always enjoyed being on the water."

Preston stared at his feet. Dad was right, but being treated by a man who might possibly be courting his former girlfriend did not appeal to him. "Yes, I want to get well, but I doubt he'd know how to treat something that's all in my head. Maybe there's someone in Chicago who can help me."

"You don't know unless you try. Doctor Murphy might be at tomorrow's wedding. If you attend, you could ask him for a recommendation."

Meet him while Maureen is on his arm as his date? He couldn't trust himself to keep his fists in his pockets, even at Katie Quinn's wedding. "I didn't intend on going to the ceremony. I've already sent my regrets. I doubt they'd want me there anyway after the way I treated her."

"You're wrong, Pres. They understand you've been unstable since that episode up in Michigan. I'm sure if you change your mind they'll be happy to have you. Let's get inside. I know your mother is anxious to hear about your new job.

CHAPTER EIGHTEEN

*B*right sunlight hit Maureen's face, and she pulled the covers over her head. She'd been enjoying a wonderful daydream starring Nate. One of several she had since waking an hour earlier. This one was more a reliving of two days ago when he carried her home, and the kisses they'd shared. Wonderful sweet kisses that sent goosebumps clear to her toes. She wanted the kisses to go on and never stop. But they did stop, except for in her dreams.

"I'll have none of that on my wedding day, sister." The covers lifted and Maureen opened her eyes to see Katie grinning down at her. Her long blond braid hanging over her shoulder threatened to tickle Maureen's nose. "Breakfast is nearly ready and your presence is required."

She made a move to get up then remembered her plan. "With my sore ankle, maybe I should stay off my feet until the wedding. You don't need me with you to enjoy your breakfast."

Katie crossed to the armoire and pulled out one of the new outfits Mama had bought for Maureen to perk up her spirits—a pale pink shirtwaist with moderate mutton sleeves and a cream-colored soft skirt that fell to the ankles. Mama said it was a design suitable for golfing.

Although she'd never golfed, she had to admit she loved the outfit. But no matter how hard Mama might try, today's wedding would be her only social event for quite some time unless it involved undercover work as a detective. She'd figured out a way to keep the left side of her face hidden as much as possible while next to Katie during the ceremony. Following that part of the day, she planned to use her sore ankle as an excuse and retreat to the veranda where she'd sit in the shadows and watch the frivolity.

The fragrance of cinnamon wafted into her room and her stomach growled. She wasn't about to miss cinnamon rolls, and as long as it was family only, she could indulge. She climbed out of bed, hobbled to the washstand, and poured water into the bowl. "I'm sorry for being a sourpuss on the most exciting day of your life, sis."

Katie hung the clothing on a wall hook and walked over to her sister. "I understand, Mo. You've been through a lot. I know you don't believe it, but God has a plan for your life. Just lean on Him and trust. He will provide.

By the time Maureen had washed up and dressed, the family had gathered in the formal dining room instead of the large kitchen table where they usually ate their morning meal.

Making sure she hobbled enough to convince them her ankle still hurt, she entered the room. Da sat at the head of the table. He leaned over and pushed back the empty chair to his left. "Sit here. We've been waiting to say the blessing on this most beautiful day when our precious Katie will become a beautiful bride. The first of my three daughters to leave the nest."

Maureen sat and spread her napkin on her lap.

"What do you mean by leave the nest, Da?" Doreen asked.

Da's blue eyes twinkled. "It's just a saying referring to when children grow up and leave home to begin their own families."

The little girl grinned. "Oh. Like when the mama bird teaches her babies how to fly and when they are strong enough they fly off."

Da beamed. "That's right. For an eight-year-old, you are a smart little girl." He bowed his head. "Let's pray."

A minute later, Da said "Amen," and Doreen grinned at Maureen. "I guess you and Doctor Murphy will be next."

Heat filled Maureen's face.

Mama stared at the child. "Doreen! Where on earth did you get that idea?"

"Two days ago, when I was playing near the shore path I saw Doctor Murphy carrying Maureen and they were kissing."

Maureen pushed out a smile and ignored the five pairs of eyes fixated on her. "I thought little sisters were to be silent at the table. I was only giving Doctor Murphy a kiss of gratitude for carrying me home after I hurt my ankle." She reached for the basket of cinnamon rolls, took one, and set it on her plate. "Richard, can you please pass me the bacon?"

Her brother snickered and opened his mouth to answer.

"Richard, do as your sister asked please, without comment."

At Mama's command he shut his mouth and passed the platter of bacon to Maureen.

"Richard and Doreen, this conversation is not to be repeated anywhere." Da looked at Maureen. "We'll talk later."

She nodded. That was what she was afraid of. As much as Mama had been pushing her to throw her affections to Nate, and Da had said to do as her heart led, at the moment, her heart was very confused. If she loved Preston like she thought, would she have enjoyed kissing Nate as much as she did?

Her appetite gone, she picked up a piece of bacon and went through the motions of nibbling at it. The wedding wasn't until one o'clock and she intended to spend the hours before the ceremony out of sight except for getting into her dress and having her hair styled.

PRESTON BUTTONED his vest and slipped his arms into the suit coat grateful it was an afternoon wedding and formal wear wasn't expected. He checked his image in the mirror over his dresser. Would Mo like his beard or prefer him clean shaven? Didn't matter what she thought. He picked up the felt derby he'd purchased last year.

The thought of seeing Maureen for the first time since that train ride from Chicago made him nervous, but not as much as the boat ride he was about to endure. He yearned to sneak a few swigs from the bottle he had buried in his dresser drawer. But if Dad caught a whiff, he'd have a lot of explaining to do. He could only hope his father didn't notice the depletion of his liquor supply.

He'd discovered a couple belts of whisky when he got home from work helped him sleep during the day. He'd planned to replenish the supply that morning before his parents arrived but when Mate interrupted him at the store, he'd forgotten.

He'd tried to convince Dad to take the phaeton to the wedding, but dad insisted going by boat was best. It would give the steam yacht's motor a good run before it was stored for the winter, and it would be easier to find a spot to tie up on Safe Refuge's pier than to find room for the carriage on the estate's property.

Dad was right, of course, although he wondered if his father wasn't making him endure the boat ride to help him overcome his irrational fears. If he sat inside the cabin and kept his focus on the floor and not the water, he might be okay.

He descended the stairs and found his parents waiting. "It's

about time you came down. I was about to come and get you."
His father turned toward the door. "Let's go."

A few minutes later, his stomach in knots, Preston climbed aboard the *Ida* and followed his mother into the cabin. It felt weird to not ask to take the wheel, but he was grateful Dad didn't insist he give it a try. They'd arrive at Safe Refuge in about ten minutes. If he couldn't stand up to his fear for that short period of time he was beyond hope.

aureen stood in front of her bedroom mirror and patted her hair. Mama's hairdresser did a beautiful job arranging her curls around her face in a way that helped mask some of the scarring. The rest of her curls were gathered and lifted to her crown. And by inserting the spray of rosebuds on the left side of her face, people's focus would be away from the scars. She lifted the chiffon scarf that matched the soft yellow of her satin dress and laid it over her head. By arranging the scarf to drape slightly over the bad side of her face, the damage was not near as noticeable.

Katie had objected to the scarf at first but agreed when she realized how self-conscious Maureen felt. When the chiffon grazed her cheek, it felt rough against the tender skin, but it that was easier to endure than people's stares.

A knock came at the door and Mama stepped in, looking as beautiful as ever with her green eyes sparkling and her hair swept up into a cloud of curls at the back of her head "Nate is downstairs. He brought something for you I think you'll like."

"What did he bring me?"

Mama smiled. "You'll have to come and see for yourself. Do

you need help getting down the stairs?"

She shook her head. "If I hold onto the bannister, like I did this morning, I think I'll be okay." It wasn't a total lie. The ankle *was* still a bit tender.

As she descended the stairs, Nate turned from where he waited by the entry hall window. Seeing him in his black cutaway sack coat, patterned trousers, and ascot tie, her heart fluttered.

He grinned. "Who is this picture of beauty coming toward me?"

A warm feeling flowed over her and she flashed him a smile. "You're looking quite handsome yourself."

He set his derby on a side table then scrambled up the steps and took hold of her elbow. "Easy now. Once step at a time."

They arrived at the bottom and he ran his gaze from her face to her satin opera slippers peeking out from under her hem. He looked her in the eyes, "Maureen, I've always said you've never lost your beauty, but today you are especially lovely."

She lowered her eyes then peered up at him through her lashes. "You're not just saying that to cheer me up, are you?"

"I'd never say anything I don't mean." He lifted the scarf from her cheek, then ran the back of his fingers over her scarred jaw, sending tingles down her neck. "Very ingenious, but you really don't need it." He let the fabric fall, and she rearranged it. "I don't plan to wear it except during the ceremony."

"Good." He picked up his hat and offered his elbow. "Now come with me to the porch and you'll see my surprise."

She took his arm and leaned on him, letting him set the pace to the veranda door. They stepped out, and she glanced about. "I don't see anything out of the ordinary."

He grinned and led her closer to the top of the steps. "Your dad gave me the flowers to make it more festive. It's there on the grass."

She looked where he pointed and gasped. She shouldn't have milked the sore ankle as much as she did. "It's a beautiful chair but why would I need it? I intend to stand next to Katie, not sit."

"Come closer and you'll see why." He helped her take the steps to the grass and then she understood.

"A wheelchair? I'm not an invalid, Nate. The only thing I plan to sit on that rolls is my bicycle, but not today." She offered a shy smile. "Once my physician says I am well enough."

The twinkle in his eyes faded. "I never said you were an invalid. Being on your feet at a social event after the fall you took can be very uncomfortable. I borrowed this from a patient who used it when she broke her ankle last spring. It's only temporary, I assure you. I'll be happy to be your escort as you sit in the receiving line, and then wheel you into the tent for the reception."

Feeling the hot sting of tears burning the corners of her eyes, she looked away and blinked. This kind man didn't deserve such a defiant response. She had to rid herself of this wretched attitude. This was Katie's day and she wasn't about to spoil it.

He handed her a white handkerchief.

She dabbed her eyes. "Your thoughtfulness is above and beyond your duties as my doctor. Thank you."

His hurt expression dissolved into a closed-lip smile. "I'm not here as your doctor." He chuckled. "I'm not sure what to call myself. Hopefully more than a friend. Let's say I'm your escort for the day, if you'll have me."

Where had their easy camaraderie of the other day gone? Did he not realize how much he'd come to mean to her? "I'd love to have you as my date today, which I think sounds better than escort, but I really don't intend on mixing with the crowd after the ceremony. As much as I'd love your company, sitting on the veranda most of the day might be boring for you."

He grinned. "I'm never bored with you, Maureen." He took her hand and squeezed it, then leaned down and pressed a kiss to her cheek. Butterflies erupted in her stomach. The day was turning out to be far better than she'd thought.

A voice she knew well sounded from the lakeshore.

Preston? He wasn't supposed to be there. She turned and stared at the familiar form standing next to his parents. Even his wool frockcoat couldn't conceal the broad shoulders and muscular arms she enjoyed seeing in plain view whenever they'd swam together off one of their docks. They may have broken up but that didn't mean she couldn't enjoy his good looks—briefly

"Nate, can you help me get back up the stairs? The guests are already arriving, and I shouldn't be seen until the ceremony." She turned, expecting to take his arm. How had he left her side without her knowing? As she moved toward the porch stairs, her bad foot landed on the edge of a flagstone paver, and she couldn't catch her balance. Her bottom hit the ground and for the first time since bustles went out of style, she wished she'd been wearing one.

Preston scrambled up the lawn. "Maureen, are you okay?"

"Yes, except for my dignity."

He took hold of her elbow. "Let me help you up." He lifted her to her feet and she brushed grass from her skirt. Seeing no stains, she reached up to rearrange the scarf, but only felt curls. She looked at Pres in time to see his face twist into a nasty grimace. She couldn't have felt more embarrassed than if she were stark naked. She glanced around the grass. She had to find the scarf.

"Is this what you're looking for?" He held it out.

Her face heated. "Yes." She snatched the scarf from his hand and draped it into position, then angled her head so the good side faced Preston. "Nice to see you, Pres. I thought you weren't coming."

He offered a tight smile. "Mother and Dad talked me into it.

I wanted reassurance you were healthy again. You look like you're almost your old self."

"You can stop the flattery. You know I don't look like I used to."

She pulled the scarf off her cheek. "Good thing I wasn't planning to run for Harvest Queen this year."

He winced and averted his gaze. "I won't lie. It … ah …will take some getting used to."

Her gut couldn't have hurt worse than if he had stabbed it with a dagger. She replaced the scarf. "I could say the same about you and that beard. But it's not the same since I can't shave my scars off my face. I could make sure only my good side is in view when we are together. But since we've broken up, I guess that's of no concern to you."

He grimaced. "Maureen. I'm sorry. The words came out wrong. I didn't mean to hurt your feelings."

Grateful the tear she felt trailing down her scarred left cheek was masked by the scarf, she raised her chin. "Which is why you broke up with me in the first place—so you wouldn't hurt me."

"I know. I'm slowly improving. I actually managed to ride over here on the *Ida*. My first time on a boat since we took the steamship to the fair."

She looked at him her eyes wide, unable to hide her joy at his news. "You drove it?"

He pressed his lips together and shook his head. "I'm not that much improved. Dad took the wheel. I stayed in the cabin and stared at the floor the whole way. I couldn't bring myself to look at the water. But it's a start. One thing you might not know is I'm now the night watchman at the city docks. Being that close to water without actually having to be on a boat seems to be helping."

"Has any doctor ever said what it is you have?"

He looked off. "There isn't a name for it. I've heard it's similar to the shell shock men who have fought in the Civil War experienced. The only thing anyone says is that maybe time will take care of it." He returned his gaze to a spot above her head. "I just wish I knew how much time. I feel like my life is standing still while everyone else moves forward."

"Maureen." Nate's voice startled her and she spun around. "I need to help you get back inside now. Your mother's orders." How had Nate snuck up on her like that? She stifled a cringe. Now the two men in her life were breathing the same air. "Yes, of course."

Nate was already sticking his hand out to Preston. "Nate Murphy. I don't think we've met."

Preston took a step back, ignoring Nate's offered hand. "We haven't. Preston Stevens." He looked Maureen's direction in a way that reminded her of how a blind person looks at you without really seeing. "Maybe we can talk again later, Mo." He turned and sauntered across the grass toward the tent.

Preston had made the right decision by ending their relationship. As much as she would always love him as a friend, there was no way she could endure anything else. It would be like living with a powder keg. She took Nate's offered elbow. "Let's get inside."

At the top of the steps she looked up at him. "I'm sorry he was so inhospitable. He hasn't been himself in a while."

"You mentioned someone named Pres several times when you were feverish. I presume he's that person."

She gaped at him. "I said his name?"

"Yes. I thought at the time he must be a suitor of yours, but you haven't mentioned him since."

She studied her feet a moment, unsure of what to say. Best to be truthful. "We've been great friends all our lives. We thought it might turn romantic, but that's all behind us. We've moved on."

She squeezed his arm, and he laid his palm on top of her hand then leaned down and kissed her forehead. "That makes me very happy."

CHAPTER TWENTY

Inside the house, Mary Jane Corwin handed Maureen a bouquet of yellow roses and baby's breath. "You'll be the first one out after Richard walks your mother to her seat and Doreen comes behind as the flower girl. Katie is about ready. I can't wait for you to see her, Mo. She's stunning."

Maureen offered her a heart-felt smile. "It should be you carrying this bouquet. You two have been best friends since sixth grade."

Mary Jane vigorously shook her head. "I was glad to be your substitute, if necessary, but the honor is yours." She looked up at Nate. "Thank you, Doctor Murphy, for helping Maureen today."

"I'm here as a friend and not on duty. Please call me Nate. I hope it's okay to call you Mary Jane."

Her face reddened. "Of course, you may, Nate." She stuck out her hand, which he accepted with a slight bow.

Mary Jane held onto Nate's hand a tiny bit too long then fluttered her eyes. "I love your bedside manner."

Maureen had enough. "Nate, I think we need to get out to the veranda. We don't want to miss our cue."

Mary Jane let go of his hand. "Right." She shooed them toward the door. "Go."

A rustling sound interrupted. "Don't leave until you've seen me, Mo."

At Katie's command, Maureen turned, and her jaw dropped. Katie had always been her cute older sister but today as a bride, she was gorgeous.

"I'll wait for you on the veranda, Mo." Without waiting for her to respond, Nate walked away.

Katie approached while Mary Jane scurried behind her to straighten the train. The ballgown dress, not a style Maureen would have chosen for herself, was perfect for her tall willowy sister. Good thing Jake was tall too, because with Katie's long blond hair crowned on top of her head, followed by the veil, any man under six feet would be shorter than she.

Maureen came as close to the wide skirt as she could manage and leaned toward her sister to embrace her in a loose hug. "You are gorgeous, Katie. Jake is going to be speechless when he sees you."

Her sister laughed. "I hope not so speechless he can't say his vows." They air-kissed and separated. "You know, with me out of the house now, the cottage is all yours."

Maureen grimaced. "At the moment, I don't want to go in there at all. I'm sure over time I'll feel differently, but right now it's more a chamber of horrors rather than the cozy cottage it really is. I'm thinking of moving into the city anyway."

Katie's eyes widened. "And leave our beautiful Geneva Lake?"

"I'm not saying permanently, but this sickness made me realize I need to stop dreaming about the things I want to do and start living them. I plan to apply for an apprentice detective position at Pinkerton's. I want to speak with Alice Chalmers while she's here at the wedding. You do know her father was Alan Pinkerton and her brothers are running the agency now."

Katie grinned. "I didn't know, but I remember you saying when you were a girl you wanted to be a detective. I didn't realize that desire stayed with you."

"Well, it has, and I intend to follow through. If I can't get hired there, I'll figure out something as adventurous to do. No more bookkeeping jobs for me."

Katie grinned. "You should try to fulfill your greatest wish, and today I'm about to fulfill mine."

"I know, but I still can't see you as a farmer's wife. You know a lot about flowers, thanks to Da, but raising crops and taking care of cows?"

She laughed. "I can learn, and I love the farmer. I'll still be teaching at Woods School at least until we start a family."

The door to the veranda opened, and Nate poked his head through. "Maureen, we need to get you out here now. The musicians are beginning to play."

Katie gave her a little wave. "I'll see you at the end of the aisle."

Outside on the lawn, Maureen waited in the shadows, until Doreen had spread rose petals over the white carpet that had been rolled down the grassy aisle. After her little sister took her seat next to Mama, Maureen began her walk, grateful the pacing set by the classical piece played by a string quartet was perfect for her tender ankle.

Preston sat several rows behind Mama and, as he turned, their gazes locked for a moment before he looked off. A couple of rows ahead of him, Nate turned as she approached, and he grinned, his eyes twinkling with approval. A vision of her being his bride on this very spot popped into her mind. For years her girlhood wedding dream included Preston, the boy who took on life with a passion and recklessness that appealed to her. But no more. The groom in her daydream had transformed into the handsome doctor. She arrived at the head of the aisle and smiled at Jake, then turned to welcome the bride.

CHAPTER TWENTY-ONE

The moment the beaming newlyweds had made their way down the aisle, Nate rolled the wicker wheel chair to Maureen's side. "Your chariot awaits, Madam."

She glanced at the chair as if she were going to protest, then slid onto the cushioned seat. He worked to not appear as giddy as he felt and knelt to flip down the footrest, making sure her beautiful dress wasn't in the way of the wheels.

Satisfied with his work, he stood and moved behind the chair. "I think you and the family are to wait at the beginning of the aisle to receive the guests before heading for the reception tent. Are you still intent on sitting on the veranda?"

Maureen glanced up at him, not bothering to rearrange the scarf that had slipped off her face and offered him a gorgeous smile. "I know it's a shock, but I've changed my mind. I'll let you help me keep to the schedule." He loved how she was comfortable with her face exposed fully to him. Hopefully, in time she'd feel the same with everyone. He patted her shoulder.

"That's quite admirable for such a headstrong woman."

She rearranged the scarf. "I know. I have no idea how long this will last."

He loved the throaty laugh that punctuated her last sentence.

He pushed her down the aisle past the guests. As they approached Stevens, the man averted his gaze. Nate couldn't help but wonder if her former suitor had not moved on as well as Maureen had. Maureen paid no attention to Stevens, but waved at Mrs. Whimple, the church organist, who sat across the aisle. The woman glimpsed at Nate then gave Maureen a look of approval. He had no idea what that was all about, but he'd take all the approvals he could gather.

They bumped the rest of the way down the aisle, stopping once or twice when Maureen wanted to have a quick word with a friend. It pleased him that when she introduced him, she never mentioned he was her doctor and called him her date.

At the end of the aisle, Nate rolled her up next to her parents who waited with the rest of the wedding party.

Her father greeted Maureen with a wide grin. "Mo, I couldn't be prouder of you. I know that took courage, but wasn't it a beautiful ceremony?"

"It was, Da. I actually forgot myself." She moved to stand, and Nate pressed his palm on her shoulder. "You're the last one in the line. Standing in one spot for a length of time is too much for your ankle."

Her father nodded. "Nate is right." He looked at Nate. "Thanks for watching out for my girl today. You've probably noticed she inherited a strong will from her mother. It's an attribute to be appreciated, but at times it requires patience for those who love her."

And those falling in love with her. "It's my pleasure, Mr. Quinn."

He grinned. "I think it's time to stop being so formal. Please, call me Rory."

Maureen's eyes widened. "I think all this talk about love today has influenced you, Da. Nate and I are enjoying getting to know each other, but we aren't—"

"Rory, you must be one proud father of the bride today."

Mrs. Whimple approached, and Rory took one of her outstretched hands.

Maureen looked up at Nate and took his hand. "Da's a little emotional today. Don't pay him any mind. And don't feel you need to stay now that I'm situated for a while."

At her touch, tingles radiated up his arm. "He speaks more truth than you might realize. I'm right where I want to be."

A few minutes later, Nate greeted one of his patients and stepped aside to have a quick private conversation. When he returned to his spot, Maureen stood next to her chair conversing with a handsome looking couple. The attractive dark-haired woman gripped Maureen's hand, "Katie is a beautiful bride. They look so happy."

"I can assure you they are." Maureen tilted her head. "Did I understand correctly that your father was Alan Pinkerton?"

Nate's jaw dropped and he quickly closed it. How in the world did Maureen know this was the founder of the Pinkerton Detective Agency's daughter?

The woman's face lit up. "Yes, he was. Not many people realize that."

"I don't know where I heard it," Maureen said. "But I've admired Pinkertons for a long time, and ever since reading about Kate Warne, I've dreamed of becoming a detective."

The woman's eyes rounded. "They do hire women for investigative work, but ..." Her gaze went to the empty wheelchair. "I'm not certain how you could be able to do that kind of work if you need a wheelchair."

Maureen's face pinked. "Oh, this is only temporary. I took a nasty fall the other day and sprained my ankle. I'm also still a little weak from a bout of smallpox. She glanced at Nate. "In fact, this is Doctor Nate Murphy, my doctor and date. It was his good care that helped me recover."

"Nate, this is Joan Chalmers and that's her husband who is talking with Da."

He and Mrs. Chalmers exchanged polite nods, then she returned her focus to Maureen. "Oh, I'm so sorry for my presumption about the wheelchair."

A corner of Maureen's mouth lifted, and she waved a dismissive hand. "No need to apologize. I understand your brothers are running the agency now. How would I contact either of them about my becoming an apprentice detective?"

"I really don't know. But my brothers would be a good place to start. How about I telephone them on Monday and tell them about you. When do you expect to apply?"

"Probably within the month."

Nate's heart fell. Had he heard right? He shouldn't have been surprised. She already told him she wasn't cut out for desk work.

"My father was quite proud of Kate Warne," Mrs. Chalmers said. "He encouraged me at one point to think about coming on board as a detective, but I wasn't interested. My brothers do enjoy it though. Feel free to contact me before you go and I'll remind them of you."

Maureen's grin could have lit up the tent all by itself. "Thank you so much."

As the Chalmers's moved on to join the crowd assembling on the lawn, Maureen sat in her chair. "Nate, did you hear that conversation? She's going to put in a word for me with her brothers who run Pinkertons."

He worked to disguise his disappointment. "I was distracted by a patient but did hear most of the discussion. You really are serious about this detective business, aren't you? I recall your mentioning maybe working in one of the smallpox infirmaries in the city. What happened to that desire?"

Her frown quickly transformed into a smile. "I'm interested in doing that too, but according to what I've read, eventually the outbreaks will lessen and caretakers won't be in demand. This is for the long term. I suppose you think only men should be doctors like you or lawyers or detectives."

"No. It's not that at all. Can we talk about this later? Here comes Sheldon Sturges and his wife to greet you."

He nodded at the couple and stepped back, allowing Maureen to carry on the conversation without him. He needed a moment to gather himself. She had mentioned her dream of becoming a detective for Pinkertons, but he never thought she'd actually go through with it, especially since their relationship was moving forward so fast. He had planned to give the current situation a couple of more weeks then ask Rory for permission to enter a courtship with Maureen, but he needed to rethink that now.

"Nate, the reception line is over. I need to be at the family's table in the tent.

He snapped out of his thoughts and stepped toward Maureen. "I'm sorry. How long were you trying to get my attention?"

She rested her index finger on her chin and tilted her head. "Oh, let's see. Maybe five minutes?"

His mouth fell open. "I guess I was in deeper contemplation than I thought."

She let out a giggle. "I'm teasing you. It wasn't more than a couple of seconds. What in the world were you thinking about? I've never seen your face so serious."

"Things about work. The other family members have already gone ahead. Let's get you over to the tent." He released the brakes on the chair and wove her in and around the circles of friends and family members. Inside the tent, they came up to the long lace-covered family table, beautifully appointed with a bouquet of white and yellow roses at either end.

Rory waved them over and indicated two empty seats to his left. "These are for you two."

Nate had assumed he would be standing in the crowd along with the other guests.

Maureen smiled up at him. "I'm glad Da agreed you should sit with me since you're my date. Maybe we can put the chair behind us along the side of the tent." She stood and he walked her to the seat next to her father.

After situating the wheelchair where Maureen had suggested, he settled in the seat next to her at the same time the servers were setting platters of small sandwiches and pitchers of iced tea on the table. Later, the family would have a private celebration supper in the house before sending the happy couple on their way to spend the night in their new home.

While the family nibbled on their food, guests wandered up to wish the newlyweds well and to say additional words to the others. With so many interruptions he doubted anyone had much to eat.

Rory clinked his spoon on his water glass and stood. "On behalf of both families, we appreciate all of you spending part of your day to celebrate Katie's and Jake's marriage. The couple is about to cut the wedding cake, and I invite all of you to gather round the cake table."

Nate hadn't realized Katie and Jake had already walked over to the table. He looked at Maureen. "Do you want to join the others while they cut the cake?"

She shook her head. "I'd rather stay here and enjoy your company. I already ate too much and cannot fathom eating cake right now. This dress is already too tight."

He set his glass of tea on the table. "And it looks beautiful on you, I might say." He took her hand, loving how well it fit into his own and squeezed it. Encouraged by her smile and by the absence of her parents for a few minutes, he leaned over ready to kiss her on the cheek.

"Mo, I owe you an apology."

They both jumped and Nate sat back and stared at Stevens.

She blinked. "Why do you need to apologize? Whatever for?"

"What I said earlier was hurtful, and I'm sorry."

She shook her head. "You already apologized. No need to do so again."

"You're very kind." Preston shifted his weight from one foot to the other. "But you know good and well what I said and didn't say." He glanced over at the wheelchair. "I didn't realize when you fell earlier you'd hurt yourself so bad you needed a wheelchair."

Her laugh sounded forced. "I didn't then. I fell on the shore path two days ago when Nate and I took a walk and twisted my ankle. Nate thought it was wise to not aggravate it with so much standing today. He surprised me with that lovely chair and even decorated it so it would blend in better. He's so thoughtful that way." She took Nate's hand and wove their fingers together.

Nate wanted to excuse himself and let this be the private conversation it should be. But to do so would draw even more attention.

Preston shrugged. "It must be the doctor in him."

A wistful smile filled her face. "I think he'd be that way even if he weren't a doctor. It's in his nature." She glanced at Nate and squeezed his hand, then gave him a look that said he was the only person in the world. "He's been the best doctor and friend a girl could ask for."

Nothing like listening to people discuss him as though he wasn't there. He fought against making an excuse and leaving before he said something to Stevens he'd be sorry for.

Preston looked at Maureen's plate and then at the sandwiches still on the serving platter. "Murphy, if you knew Maureen as long as me, you'd know she abhors roast beef that's still pink. She prefers it like this one." He picked up a well-done roast beef sandwich and set it on her plate. I'll leave you two to your meal. Hope to see you again soon, Mo." He turned and strode toward the exit.

Nate looked at Maureen. "Didn't you choose that rare roast beef sandwich yourself?"

"I did. I used to dislike rare roast beef when I was a youngster, but I like it that way now. I could smack him for creating an issue on Katie's wonderful day. I'm glad the rest of the family wasn't at the table." She looked him directly in the eyes. "In fact, I'm going to show everyone I have a new man in my life. She leaned over and kissed him on the lips, letting it linger a few moments.

The woman never ceased to surprise him and he was loving every minute of it.

CHAPTER TWENTY-TWO

One Week Later

Maureen sat at her vanity arranging a scarf around her head. But the wool fabric was heavier than the chiffon she'd used at the wedding and not cooperating. Though the large bonnets women wore when Mama was her age were long out of fashion, she wanted one in the worst way. Or at least have the outside temperature so cold she could wear her winter coat with the fur-trimmed hood.

Nate had asked several times since the wedding for a dinner date in town and she had come up with a viable excuse each time, suggesting they eat with the family and spend time together that way. She felt terrible saying no, especially after how he'd arranged for the wheelchair and stayed by her side the entire wedding. She giggled at the memory of how after she kissed him during the wedding reception, a murmur of gasps had filled the tent, including a loud one from Mama.

Many of the younger women came up to her later and said they loved what she did and how it put a halt on the wagging tongues about Preston and Nate nearly coming to blows, which was an exaggeration.

Yesterday, he stopped by just to see her and to take a walk. There was no need to carry her this time, but they did stop under that same tree and sit on a blanket he'd brought. She was relieved he enjoyed her surprise kiss at the wedding and loved her impetuousness. As they stood to return to the house, he pulled her into his arms and kissed her, then asked her for a dinner date for tonight. As usual, she'd suggested a dinner in, but he refused. She needed to get out of the house and back into normal living.

He was right, and she had to at least give it a try. She could be with him without feeling self-conscious about the scarring, but could she be as comfortable out in public among people who knew her before her looks changed? The moment of truth had arrived.

The doorbells chimed from downstairs, followed by Da's voice as he greeted Nate. She listened to the men laughing and chatting. She'd never heard Da carry on in such an amiable way with Preston or any other young man she'd gone out with, most of whom he'd known since they were children. She felt like a schoolgirl heading out for her first date. In a way it was. The first date for the new Maureen Quinn, scars and all.

Da appeared in her open door. "Nate's here for you, Mo."

She turned and his face lit up. "You look lovely, a picture of your mama when she was your age."

She rolled her eyes. "You know that's not true. Not anymore."

"What do you mean?"

"You know as well as I do, I no longer look like Mama. Her skin is still flawless."

Da closed the space between them and wrapped his arms around her. "My dear daughter, a few scars on your face has done nothing to diminish the beautiful woman you've become."

She pressed her face to his chest and hugged him back. "You're prejudiced because you're my father."

He leaned back and smiled. "I beg to differ, but this is a lesson you need to learn for yourself. Nate mentioned he's taking you to Kaye's Resort for dinner. I told him to take the *Doreen* rather than using his phaeton. Much quicker. I already checked out the boat's engine and gas lighting. All is in good shape. Go and have a good time."

She whispered her thanks, grateful that at least by going to Kaye's, there would be more people she didn't know than had they gone to a restaurant in town. She made another try to arrange the scarf, but it slipped off her cheek again. She pulled it off her head and tossed it onto a chair, then headed for the door. She stopped at the top of the staircase, pushed out a smile, and descended the stairs.

Handsome in his dark wool suit and ascot tie that was becoming popular with the men, Nate grinned as she came down the steps. "There's my beautiful date."

"Oh, how you flatter me." She reached the bottom of the staircase and he stepped closer and ran the backs of his fingers over the damaged cheek as he'd taken to doing, then bent and feathered a soft kiss on the gnarled skin. "No scarf tonight?"

"It kept falling off."

He smiled. "You okay going out without it?"

"It's time I get used to it. Da said he suggested we take the *Doreen* to Kaye's." She stepped to the hall tree, but before she could reach for her black cape, he beat her to it and lifted the garment from its hook. "I presume this is yours?"

She nodded and turned so he could slip it over her shoulders. As he arranged the cape's ruffled neck trim, his fingertips grazed her skin then stayed there.

"Your skin feels so soft, Mo."

"My neck isn't scarred?"

He placed his hands on her shoulders and turned her to face him. "Nary one mark."

She dropped her gaze. "At least two parts of me looks normal."

"There's more than two parts."

She'd almost forgotten that as her doctor he'd seen just about all her parts usually only viewed by a woman's husband. At least if she married him, he would find no surprises on their wedding night. A flush of heat filled her face. They had to change the subject, and she needed to get her thoughts out of where they didn't belong. "Shall we go?"

"Yes. You're adorable when you blush, by the way."

Wouldn't he be surprised at what had caused her to redden?

He led the way through the home's center hall and out to the veranda. Maureen gasped. "Everything looks pink—the sky, the trees, even the lake.

"It's the sunset. It was starting on my way over here. I wonder why the sunsets are so brilliant in an autumn sky. It must be something in the atmosphere."

She took Nate's arm. "It's almost as if you ordered it for us. What a wonderful night for a cruise across the lake."

He laid his palm over her hand and smiled down at her. "It's obviously good medicine for you."

A few minutes later, they got the steam yacht started, and Nate expertly captained it away from the dock and turned the vessel toward the south shore halfway down the length of the lake. He settled back on the bench behind the wheel and patted the cushion beside him. "There's room for both of us. Come sit next to me."

Maureen grinned, remembering the many times growing up when she'd cuddle next to Da while he piloted their boat. If Mama was along, the spot next to Da was reserved for her. She'd loved those times with her father and after her crush on Preston had emerged, she often dreamed of doing the same with him in his boat. She slid onto the seat, enjoying how it was just wide enough for the two of them. Nate wrapped his arm around her waist and lowered the speed. "We're in no hurry when we have such a wonderful view of God's handiwork."

"I had no idea you knew how to pilot this kind of boat."

He grinned. "One of the first things I did when I arrived here last spring was to take lessons because it's my hope to own a steam yacht someday. Mate Napper was one of my first patients, and when I suggested he give me lessons in lieu of payment, he readily agreed. What a blessing from the Lord those lessons were."

"That's how Mr. Napper recognized you when he saw us after I fell." She looked up at him. "I've seen you in church a number of times, but never heard you speak of God before."

"Sure, you have. When you were feverish and restless, I often came to your bedside and prayed out loud for God to heal you and to help me take care of you. You always said 'Amen' along with me."

"I don't remember but thank you for doing that."

"I pray over all my patients, by the way, not just for you." If she were able to gauge her feelings for him like one would measure the temperature, the mercury had just sprung up at least ten degrees.

He pulled her closer into the crook of his arm and kissed her, his lips so soft. She slipped her arm across his back and rested her head on his shoulder. Such a different boat ride from the last one she'd taken with Pres. This was how it was supposed to be.

Even traveling at a slow speed, they reached the Kaye's Resort dock before the sun had dropped completely out of sight behind the trees. A young man from the resort assisted in tying the ropes to cleats attached to the pilings, then helped Maureen as she transferred to the pier. Nate joined her and she slipped her hand around his proffered arm.

As they reached the shore and started up the walk toward the large dining room, Nate glanced at her. "Are you still okay being in a public dining room?"

Feeling like she could take on the world as long as this man was beside her, she nodded. "I'll be fine as long as you're with me."

He covered her hand with his and squeezed. "I love hearing you say that. I can't think of anywhere I'd want to be but alongside of you.

CHAPTER TWENTY-THREE

They strolled hand in hand down the gaslight-lit walkway toward the resort's dining room. It had been a long time since Maureen felt this happy. "I used to love coming here. But between working at the furniture store and doing other things on weekends, time got away from me. Have you come here often?"

"I discovered the resort soon after I moved here. The summer season had already begun and I often took the *Commodore* here on Saturday mornings and returned the last trip that evening. Most enjoyable. We had nothing like this in Columbus."

"You never said what town you grew up in."

"A small town in Ohio called Springfield. Growing up, I used to love going to a small lagoon in Snyder Park where people could rent rowboats in summer and ice skate in winter. I could only afford to rent a boat a few times, but it was fun watching them, especially when someone fell in."

"Oh no. Wasn't that dangerous?"

"I suppose so, but to a kid it was funny. As far as I know, no one ever got hurt."

"What brought you to Lake Geneva?"

"Since my mother passed away before I graduated medical college, I had no reason to stay in Ohio. Someone told me Doctor Kiley was planning to retire and was seeking someone to take over his practice. I contacted him, then took the train to Lake Geneva last spring. As soon as I saw the lake and village, I was sold."

Her heart sank. She was very fond of Nate, but if she married him, she'd likely spend the rest of her life without realizing her dream. Did she love him enough to change her life's direction? "Here you are excited to be living here, while I can't wait to get to the city and start my next adventure."

He stopped walking and looked down at her. "Like becoming a detective with Pinkertons?"

"If they will have me, yes. Think of it, Nate. I could be assigned a situation out west on the frontier, tracking down stagecoach robbers and protecting the passengers."

"Sounds exciting." He started them walking again.

How could she expect him to understand? For years she couldn't wait to be old enough to go off on her own, with or without her parents' blessings. Now she had her chance. "Mama always tells me I am more like her sister, Callie, than her. I sometimes feel like I'm caught between two worlds. My friends from town who expect to live here all their lives and those who live in the city during the winter and attend colleges in the east. Several have actually moved to Great Britain to explore the idea of making a match with a British Lord."

"That doesn't appeal to you?"

"Not really. Even if it did, the trust from my granddaddy isn't large enough for that kind of situation. I still believe in love being the key to a happy marriage. Like what my parents have."

"Here we are at the dining room. Shall we go in?" Nate opened the door and held it for her.

She had much more to say as she entered and hoped to continue the conversation at their table.

A distinguished looking man wearing a black suit and bow tie greeted them with a slight bow. "Good evening and welcome to Kaye's. A table for two?"

"Yes. We have reservations. The name is Murphy."

The man stepped to a podium and glanced at a paper. "Ah, hear it is."

Nate handed the man a dollar. "Can you please seat us away from the piano so we can talk without the music making it hard to hear?"

The host slipped the bill into his pocket. "Of course. Doctor and Mrs. Murphy, please come this way."

Maureen caught Nate's eye as he opened his mouth, she presumed to correct the man. She shook her head and he pressed his lips together. No use embarrassing the fellow. She followed the man into the dining room with Nate coming behind, keeping his hand on the small of her back. They stepped past several tables filled with diners and crossed to a far corner of the room. The host stopped beside a table in front of a tall Palladian window. "I hope this will be sufficient for your comfort. You just missed a beautiful sunset. The view here was magnificent."

"We enjoyed the sunset during our boat ride over. It was wonderful and this table looks perfect," Nate replied.

The host pulled out one of the chairs and nodded at Maureen. "Madam?" She sat while the man pulled out the chair across from her and nodded at Nate. Nate placed a hand on the chair to her right. "I'd prefer to sit here."

"Of course, Doctor." The host scurried toward the chair, but Nate had already taken his seat. Within a couple of moments, the man had moved the place setting from the other position until it was in front of Nate, then handed them both a menu. "Would you like to place your drink orders now?"

They both ordered iced tea and the man scurried off.

Maureen giggled and leaned toward Nate. "Thank you. I would have hated having you across the table from me. It's very difficult to talk that way."

"Thanks for stopping me from correcting him earlier about presuming we were married."

She laughed. "Don't think I wasn't tempted to say something, but It didn't seem important enough to cause him embarrassment."

He took her hand and gave it a squeeze. "I love your sensitivity to things like that."

A waiter appeared with their teas a few minutes later, and after they gave their orders—baked whitefish in champagne sauce for Maureen and beef short ribs in gravy for Nate—she glanced around the crowded restaurant. "I'm surprised they are this busy during the week now that the children are back in school."

Nate scanned the room. "I hadn't thought about that, but it is surprising."

The waiter appeared with their appetizer, a broth soup with the vegetables cut into thin julienne slices. Somehow an awkward tension had pervaded and she was grateful for the soup to have something to do besides casting about for something to say. She lifted her soup spoon.

"Do you mind if I say a blessing first?"

She set the spoon on the table. They never had a meal at home without Da saying grace first, but not ever had she seen it done at a restaurant. "Of course not. Go ahead."

He bowed his head, and she did the same. He spoke so low she barely heard his words. He said "Amen" before she had time to feel self-conscious, and she raised her head. "That was a new experience."

He grinned. "Most people don't bless their meals outside of

their homes, but I started doing it a few years ago. I rather like giving the example of being thankful for my food."

"I thought it was nice." She picked up her spoon. Different but nice.

The meal courses arrived, and Nate withdrew further into his meal. By the time they started on their green apple pies for dessert, she couldn't wait to finish and get back to the boat.

Her appetite for the dessert gone, she pushed a bite-sized piece of pie around her plate. "Nate, can I ask you something?"

He looked up after forking a bite of pie. "Of course."

"Why have you been so quiet? Usually we can't stop talking whenever we're together, but it seems your meal has taken all your attention."

He laid his fork on his plate and reached for her hand. "I'm sorry, Maureen. You caught me off guard with all that talk about chasing bad guys in the west. I can't get a vision of you hunting down a gang of robbers and getting into a gun fight. But, it's something else you said that stole the words I planned to say tonight."

She frowned. "What did I say?"

"That you plan to move to Chicago no matter the outcome at Pinkertons. I thought you loved living here. And what about your job at the furniture store?"

She blinked. "I do love it here. As for the job, I never intended it to be my life's work, and they couldn't leave it open for more than a couple of weeks. Just as well, because I have dreams that can't be fulfilled if I stay. If I learned one thing from being sick, it's that we have to seize the moment and not keep putting off what we sense we are to do with our lives."

"I thought you wanted a family and children. Isn't that what most women want?"

"I want that eventually. But I don't see that it has to be one way or the other. Why can't it be both? I'm certain that if I marry, I can both work outside the home and take care of my family at the same time. No matter if it's being a detective or something else. Raising a family would be one part of my life and working at a career would be the other."

His eyes widened. "What's wrong with being at home full time to raise a family?"

"There's nothing wrong with it. But a woman can be more if she wants. Are you aware Lake Geneva has a female dentist?"

"Yes. I went to Dr. Sherman last month for a toothache."

"Did she tell you she's married and has a child?"

"Yes. But she doesn't have to travel into dangerous situations like what you described."

"That's true." She lifted her shoulders and let them drop. "I haven't worked it all out yet. All I know is that I need to at least explore the idea. If it doesn't work out, it doesn't work out."

He pushed the remains of his pie around his plate. "If you feel this way, why did you give me the impression you are interested in me?"

She stared at her lap. It was a fair question, but she wasn't ready to answer it. How could she when she wasn't sure Nate understood her? She raised her head. "Lately, my dreams have been about a certain ginger-haired doctor whom I have come to be very fond of. It may take my going to the city for a while to sort it out."

He picked up the bill from the table, then pulled out his bill-fold and laid several dollars on top of it. "I've left plenty to cover our meals and the tip. Let's get out of here."

He helped her into her cape, giving her shoulders a slight squeeze as he did so. Outside, he took her hand and guided her a direction other than the way to the dock. "Has it gotten too chilly to sit a few minutes and talk? There's a gazebo up ahead."

Relief washed over her. She'd been certain she'd talked herself out of any hope she had of furthering a relationship with Nate. "I'd like that."

At the gazebo they sat on one of the benches and he put his

arm around her. "Maureen, I am not a stick-in-the-mud kind of man. There were a couple of women who graduated from medical college with me, both married and one was expecting. I never thought they had no business being there, and they both are practicing medicine today. I guess I assumed since you were raised on this beautiful lake, that you would want the same kind of life that your family has had." He took her hand and wove their fingers together. "I planned to ask you tonight if we could officially court with the expectation of getting engaged in the spring. I asked your father for permission when we had lunch yester—"

"You asked my father for my hand?" She leaned back and stared at him.

"I wasn't talking about getting engaged. Just permission to exclusively date you, or court you as it's called where I come from."

As forward thinking as she tended to be, she loved the idea of courting. Wasn't that when one agreed to be in an exclusive relationship with the shared goal of making sure they were a good match for marriage? "Some couples court around here too. What did he say?" She barely heard her own voice she said it so low.

"He was surprised but quite happy to agree if it was your desire." He softly chuckled. "He did warn me you can be impetuous."

"Which you already knew. Was that all he said?"

"He said someone else might figure in your decision, but he hoped not because the other man wouldn't be a good match."

"Preston."

"The man who interrupted our meal at the wedding?"

"Yes. It was one of those things when you're little you say you're going to marry your playmate when you grow up. That's how it's been for both of us. I do hold a deep affection for him, but he's quite messed up in the head and nowhere near being ready to settle down. It's over between us." She squeezed his hand. "I'm very attracted to you, Nate. Courting sounds too locked in place this early in our knowing each other. Can we agree to see only each other over the next several months without giving what we have an official name and see how it goes?"

He gathered her into his arms and kissed her. "Is that answer enough or do you need words?"

She pressed her face against his chest and hugged him. "Words are nice, but your kisses are nicer. Thank you for understanding." *But did he really?*

CHAPTER TWENTY-FOUR

The next morning Maureen slept until half past nine, surprised Mama didn't come to find out if she were ill. When Nate brought her home from Kaye's Resort, they'd stayed on the boat talking a while longer. The more he'd talked, the more she realized he was the kind of man she needed. Reason told her that she should tell him yes, she'd like for him to court her, but an unsettled feeling stopped her.

At one point not long ago if Preston had suggested they run off and get married, she wouldn't have hesitated. She was certain then that she loved Pres with all her heart, and now she realized that what she thought was love was more of an infatuation based on his good looks and sense of adventure. Or was it.

Preston's look of disgust when he first saw her scars had left her cold. He'd known her all her life, and yet it seemed his affection was based on looks, not what was in her heart. She couldn't help what other people thought but Preston wasn't just anyone. She threw back the covers and climbed out of bed. Time to make him own up to her. If he worked last night at the watchman job he should be home by now.

She dressed in a plain skirt and shirtwaist and scurried

down the stairs. In the kitchen, Mama sat at the table talking with Aunt Callie who had been staying with the family for a visit following the wedding. Maureen crossed the room to the tea kettle that sat over a low flame on the stove and made of cup of tea. "I'll eat later. I have something I need to do first."

"Can't it wait, Maureen?" Aunt Callie asked. "Robert and I are heading back to Evanston on the noon train. We plan to leave here early enough to stop in town to visit an old classmate of mine. I may not be here when you return."

If she waited, she might lose her courage. "I really can't, Aunt Callie. Maybe I can come by and see you when I come to the city in a couple of weeks."

A smile filled her aunt's features. Never as beautiful as her mother, Aunt Callie had a spunk that Maureen admired. "Oh, we'd love to have you stay with us. The trolley is only a quick trip downtown, which I'm sure is where you'd prefer to be rather than stuffy old Evanston. Although the university campus has some handsome young men." She winked while Mama made a face.

"You've hardly changed, sister dear, Mama said. "Maureen already has a young man."

Aunt Callie's brows rose into perfect arches. "Really? I thought she and Preston were through."

"Not him."

"You don't mean that handsome doctor who wheeled her around at the wedding."

"That's the one." Mama beamed.

An impish grin filled Aunt Callie's features. "Then it's true what I heard."

"What did you hear?" Mama asked.

"That while I was still by the cake that Maureen had kissed the doctor right there in front of everyone."

Mama rolled her eyes. "I'm afraid my impulsive daughter takes more after you than me. Yes. It's true."

Aunt Callie looked over at Maureen. "My dear niece, you have a wonderful taste in men. But I always thought you and Preston would end up together." She frowned. "I've never seen him so sullen as he was at the wedding."

Until now Aunt Callie was the only one in her corner regarding Preston, and now even she had changed her mind.

"Thank goodness she isn't with him anymore," Mama said."

Maureen let out a sigh. "Talk all you want about me. The both of you are going to be very disappointed because I'm on my way to visit Preston."

Both pairs of jaws dropped open and Maureen laughed. "Shut your mouths. I'm going to give him a piece of my mind for pretending I don't exist now that my face is scarred."

"He ignored you?" The sisters asked in unison.

"First, he made a horrible face when he saw the scarring. Then while Nate and I stayed at the table while the cake cutting was going on he came up to us and acted like a petulant child. He's the one who broke up with me but acts as though I'm not allowed to see anyone else." She set her empty cup on the sink. If I'm not back within the hour, send out a search party."

"How are you getting there?" Mama asked.

"I'm thinking of using the phaeton, if that's okay."

Mama waived her hand. "Go. Your father will be taking Callie and Robert to the train in the carriage."

AT SHELTER BAY, Maureen was relieved that Dusty was in the small pen next to the stable. She hitched her horse to a post and crossed the grass to the stately brick home's back door. She knocked several times without a response and was about to try the door when it opened, and a strong odor of whisky wafted over her.

She stared up into Preston's bleary eyes. "Whew. You smell like you've been on an all-night binge."

He kept his gaze somewhere over her shoulder and leaned to one side, then righted himself and leaned against the door frame. "If you came over here to criticize, you can turn around and go home." He started to close the door, but she wedged her boot against the doorjamb then pushed past him. She headed for the kitchen and began opening cupboard doors. "Where do you keep the coffee?"

He stumbled into the room. "Don't have any. But I have plenty of whisky, if you want that."

She spun around. "That's the last thing I want. The coffee was for you to get you sober. Were you drinking while you were at work?"

He dropped into a chair and ran his fingers through his thick disheveled hair. "There's nothing else to do there but drink. That dock is the most boring place. Whisky helps pass the time."

She glanced around. "Are your parents here?"

"They left the day after the wedding. Do you think I'd come home in this state if they were?"

"At least that shows some sense."

He produced a small flask from his pants pocket and put it to his lips. He took a couple of swallows and tried to recap the container.

Unable to watch his feeble attempts, Maureen grabbed the bottle. "Give me the cap."

He stared at her outstretched hand.

"Give it to me, Pres."

He sighed and handed her the cap. She screwed it onto the bottle then kept hold of it.

"Hey, give it to me."

"Look at me, and then I'll give it to you."

He continued to look past her shoulder. "I am looking at you."

"No, you're not. Look at my face."

He didn't move.

"Look at my face. Look at my scars."

He shook his head. "I can't."

"You can't or you won't?"

"Both."

"Why can't you?"

"You don't need to know."

"Please, Pres, look at me."

He crossed his arms. "No."

"Look at me! Why won't you look at me?" Her raised voiced echoed about the room.

Tears rolled down his grizzled jaw. "Because I can't stand to. Your beautiful face is gone just like the boy I tried to save. All our dreams are gone. You've moved on to Nate. Go back to him and leave me alone." He stood and snatched up the bottle.

She didn't move until she heard his heavy footfalls going upstairs. Her heart ached for him, yet she knew no way to help him. "God, You can help him. Please don't leave him in the sorry mess he's become. He may not be the man for me, but he's still my friend." She palmed away her tears and stood.

Outside, she headed for the stable, found hay and tossed it on the thinning grass in the pen. She then checked the water trough and added a bucketful from the faucet. That should get Dusty through until Preston would leave for his job. Assuming he sobered up enough to go. The men at the livery where Preston boarded him in town would see to Dusty's care overnight.

She climbed in the carriage and got the horse moving toward South Shore Drive. When she arrived home, she turned the horse out into the pasture and went straight to her room. Leaning against her closed bedroom door, a large sob that had been wedged in her throat the entire ride home finally exploded. She let out a wail and fell face down on the bed.

Preston may have said he'd lost her beautiful face, but she'd lost something far worse. Her best friend. But was he her best friend if he couldn't look at her now?

A knock came at the door. "Maureen, can I come in?"

She didn't answer and another knock sounded. "Mo, if you don't answer, I'm coming in anyway."

"Come in if you must."

Her mother scurried to the bed and sat on its edge. She began rubbing a circle on Maureen's back. "Tell me what happened."

"He was drunk when I got there." She raised up on an elbow and looked at her mother. "He hates me, Mama. He refuses to look at me because I'm no longer beautiful. He says he lost me, just like he lost that little boy in the storm. He drinks at his job. Says it's boring and drinking helps pass the time."

"Oh, my sweet daughter. I'd like to go over there and wring his neck for treating you like that."

She sat up all the way. "He's sick. What he has is as bad as what I had, except I healed from mine. His doesn't seem to have an end."

Her mother's arms went around her. "I'm not going to say I told you so about him. I suppose I should alert his mother to what's happening. Maybe they already know."

"I don't think so. He said he didn't drink the days they were here. They went back to Chicago the day after the wedding. I'm guessing he's been drinking ever since. He's probably sleeping it off now." She fished a handkerchief from her skirt pocket and blew her nose. "I need to talk to someone who has experienced what I'm going through. Do you think Mrs. Ambrose would let me talk to her? She has such a wonderful attitude about handling rejection and not letting peoples' disdain bother her."

Mama's face brightened. "Maureen, that's a perfect idea. Why don't you call her and see if you might visit her? Your father would be glad to take you. She lives on the Delavan inlet. When I called to hire her for you, I gave her name to the central operator and she knew how to ring her. She's probably in high demand. There aren't many around who are able to do what she does."

"I didn't think about how she might be on a new assignment." Tears pricked her eyes. "It's going to be hard to wait until she's free if that's the case."

"Perhaps you could go to wherever she is. While her patient is sleeping, you can talk."

"That's true. I can do that since I'm inoculated."

In the kitchen, Maureen went to the telephone and turned the crank, then lifted the earpiece.

"What number do you wish?"

"Can you please connect me to Mrs. Ambrose in Delavan?"

"Of course. I hope someone else in your family hasn't come down with the pox."

Is nothing a secret around here? "No, nothing like that."

Some static came through the connection, then Mrs. Ambrose's distinctive voice came through the earpiece. "Hello, this is Beatrice Ambrose."

Maureen nodded at her mother to indicate their friend had answered. "Mrs. Ambrose, this is Maureen Quinn."

"Oh, my sweet Maureen. I've been praying for you and wondering how you are doing. Have you regained all your strength?"

She could almost hear the older woman's smile. "Yes, I'm almost as strong as before." She paused certain the operator was listening. She swallowed back a sob. "Can I come to your house so we can talk in person?"

"Of course. Of course. I just finished a case and arrived home yesterday. Can you come tomorrow morning? Why don't you stay with me a few days? Unless you don't have the time in your schedule."

"I have the time. Thank you. I have to make sure Da can bring me tomorrow. I'll let you know by the end of today."

They said their goodbyes, and she leaned against the wall, allowing the tears to flow. "She wants me to spend a few days with her. I hope Da can take me in the morning."

Mama embraced her. "If he can't, I'll get the directions to her house from him and take you myself."

She leaned back. "Have you ever gone over to Delavan before?"

"Not alone, but I've gone with your father a few times. The inlet isn't as far as the town itself. It can't be that difficult. Remember, I've been driving carriages since before the great fire and was fully prepared to do so that night to get away from the flames."

Maureen forced a smile. "You've only told me the story about two dozen times."

Her mother chuckled. "Yes, I guess I have. The memory is seared into my brain as if it happened last week."

Maureen turned the telephone's crank. "I need to call Nate and ask him to stop by after he's done seeing patients. I can't go without telling him where I'll be."

CHAPTER TWENTY-FIVE

Maureen stared into her armoire. Nate was to join them for dinner, and she needed to look halfway presentable. She should have changed into a dressing gown when she first came upstairs, but sensibility was never her strong suit and now her outfit was wrinkled. She selected a yellow shirtwaist and put it on along with a black ankle-length skirt.

Da's voice filtered up from downstairs and she quickly secured her up-do with a decorative hairpin. When she talked to Da earlier about taking her to Mrs. Ambrose's in the morning he said if he could reschedule a delivery of trees until the next day, he could take her. Otherwise, her visit with Mrs. Ambrose would have to wait until day after tomorrow.

She turned to head downstairs, but her father was already at her door. "By the smile on your face I'm assuming you were able to reschedule tomorrow's delivery?"

He nodded. "You can let Mrs. Ambrose know you'll be there around ten-thirty. We'll leave by nine-fifteen." He walked over and embraced her. "How are you doing?"

"I'm okay."

"It must have been a brutal discussion with Preston for this to come up."

She willed the tears to not reappear. "Da, it was terrible. I'm very worried about him. He'd been drinking all night. He'll lose his job if they find out he's imbibing while on duty."

A deep V formed between his brows. "Maybe it would be good for him to lose the job. He needs something to straighten him out."

"I think what's going on in his head is much deeper. I'm grateful we didn't do something foolish earlier like elope."

Her father leaned back and stared at her. "Don't tell me you had considered it."

"I know it seems fast, but remember we've been close ever since we were in diapers. Since he came home from Yale, we'd grown closer. He's the only one who understands that I'm not like other women, and although I favor Mama, I'm not like her."

His eyes twinkled. "You are more like her than you think. Tenacious is the first word that comes to mind."

"Well, there's that."

"There's more. Not willing to bow to tradition."

She smirked. "Okay so we have more in common than looks. You'd think she'd understand me."

"She does. And that's why she worries about you making snap decisions and getting hurt by them. If Pres comes around and wants to resume the relationship, please don't be impulsive."

"Da, I'm over it. I realize now my love for him is more as a best friend. Not the lasting kind of love you and mama have."

He pulled her against his chest. "I'm so relieved to hear you say that. I mean him no harm, but I have never felt he was a good match for you."

The bells to the downstairs door chimed and Maureen stepped out of Da's embrace. "That must be Nate. I plan to tell him tonight where I'll be for a few days."

"Now there's a young man I'd like to see you with."

She turned. "I am very drawn to him and I know he cares for me. But I need to figure things out before I pursue a deeper relationship with him."

He drew her into a side hug, "You're being very mature about this. I'm proud of you, Mo."

Voices sounded from downstairs as Nate was let into the house. Maureen stepped toward the door. "Thank you. I just hope by the time I return home I have some answers."

The family dinner dragged on much longer than usual with Richard taking up most of the conversation while they discussed what his science project should be for school. Fascinated with the new observatory being planned for Williams Bay to house the new 40-inch refracting telescope first seen at the Columbian exposition, Richard wanted his project to be about the telescope. But he lacked a way to travel to the University of Chicago on such short notice. Nate suggested he do a report on the microscope. That was something Nate could provide help with.

That settled they moved on to dessert. Finally, Maureen was able to pull Nate aside into Da's study for a private discussion. On the settee, she took his hand. "I wanted to tell you that I'm leaving for a few days and I don't want you to worry about me."

His eyes widened. "I suppose you're going to Chicago to apply for that job."

She shook her head. "Not at all. Da is taking me to Delevan Inlet to spend a few days with Mrs. Ambrose. I'm very confused right now, Nate. About how to deal with the way people react to my scars and how to deal with my life in general."

He hung his head. "You mean dealing with my wanting to court."

She let go of his hand and gripped both his shoulders. "That's part of it. I want to give you the right answer. I have deep feelings for you, but I'm afraid."

He locked gazes with her. "Afraid of what? I'd never hurt you if that's what you mean."

"I know that, Nate. I'm afraid of hurting you." She let her hands slide down his arms and took both his hands in her own. "I know what it's like to be hurt, and I never want to hurt you that way. Have you ever thought about how you came to have feelings for me while I was sick? Is that the right way to fall in love with a person, when they are deathly ill or maybe out of pity for their scars?"

He pressed his palm against her scarred cheek. "My dear Maureen, I loved you before you took sick."

She blinked. "But there were only two times we were together. When I sold you your dresser and later when we sat next to each other in church, but we never spoke."

He chuckled. "We never spoke, but it wasn't because of my lack of wanting to. You took off like a scared jackrabbit as soon as the last note on the organ played. My affections started when you waited on me at the furniture store. Don't you remember how long it took me to decide which dresser to buy?"

She smirked. "A very long time. I never knew a man to be so undecided about a piece of furniture. Usually if they are alone, they come in, point at one, and buy it."

He nodded. "That's me. But not that day. I wanted to prolong the time as much as possible because I'd never been so drawn to a woman as I was that day. Not only because of your beauty, but as we chatted about different things, I saw your heart and your passion for life. I wanted to know more about you. When we later sat next to each other in church I couldn't wait for the service to end so I could ask you to lunch. But as I said, you scooted away so fast I never had the opportunity."

She made a face. "And if it weren't for my mother, I might not have been so anxious to get away from you. Blame it on my rebellious tendencies."

"What does your mother have to do with it?"

Now she'd gotten herself into a fix. Did she dare admit her mother had been pushing her to set her sights on Nate? "Let's just say that mothers often think they know what's best for their children, even their adult ones. And no matter what she has suggested to me over the years, I automatically do the opposite. She had mentioned you more than once as a possible suitor for me. This is one time I regret not listening to her."

A smile split his face and he pulled her into a hug. "That's the best news I've had all day. So why are you confused and needing to talk to Bea… I mean, Mrs. Ambrose?"

"I have some issues that need sorting out beyond what I'm feeling. Trust me, Nate, I really care a lot for you in the deepest possible way."

He leaned in and brought their mouths together, his lips soft and gentle on hers and her arms went around him. Tingles trailed down her neck and her stomach flip-flopped. She'd miss him the next couple of days, but hopefully the time with Mrs. Ambrose would be worth it all.

THE NEXT MORNING, Maureen sat wrapped in a blanket next to Da as he drove his wagon toward Mrs. Ambrose's home.

He nudged his shoulder against hers. "I expect we should have taken the phaeton. You'd be a lot warmer."

"Not that much. Neither has a heater. I didn't expect it to be so chilly."

"Me either or I would have covered the roses. I'm afraid the frost has brought an end to their blooms for this year."

"You have a lot in the greenhouse, don't you?"

"Yes, but the ones grown inside are not as fragrant. At least we managed to hold Katie's wedding in time. And this freeze is a reminder I soon need to arrange to get the boat in drydock for the winter. Here's our turn." He guided the wagon onto a road and then into a drive that led to a small bungalow. Ahead, past the house and a small barn, a sliver of water flowed toward the larger Delavan Lake.

Maureen shielded her eyes with her hand. "I always wondered what the inlet was. Is that it?"

"Yes. Several creeks flow into this channel, called an inlet, and then into Delavan Lake on the other side of the road." He glanced toward the house. "There's Mrs. Ambrose."

Maureen faced the small home. The sight of the older woman waving cheerily from the small porch was just the pick-me-up she needed. She climbed out of the buggy, not waiting for Da to assist her, and scurried up the walk. "Mrs. Ambrose, I'm so happy to see you again."

Mrs. Ambrose rushed down the porch steps into Maureen's waiting embrace. "You are a sight for my old eyes. It does my heart good." She turned to greet Da. "Hello, Mr. Quinn. It's good to see you again, too, and thank you for bringing our girl to me."

"It's my pleasure. You're looking well."

She pointed toward the sky. "Thanks to the good Lord. He continues to keep me strong to care for the sick."

He turned to the wagon and tugged Maureen's small valise from the back. "Let's get Mo settled."

"I hope you can stay long enough for some tea before you head back to your work."

"I wouldn't mind. Hot tea sounds good on this chilly morning."

After a short visit, Maureen walked her father out to the wagon.

He drew her into a last hug. "Your mother and I will be praying for you. Let me know when you're ready to come home and I'll be here as soon as I can."

"I'm sure it won't be but a few days."

He placed a kiss on her forehead then climbed onto his

bench and picked up the reins. "Bye for now, my sweet daughter."

She waited until the carriage turned off Mrs. Ambrose's lane onto the road, then stepped inside her hostess's cozy parlor.

Mrs. Ambrose emerged from a hallway on the right. "I put your bag in the guest room. Let me show you where it is, and we can talk after you've settled in."

Down the short hall, Mrs. Ambrose opened one of two closed doors. "I wish it were larger, but it's comfortable."

Maureen entered the room. Hard against the wall in the far corner, a quilt-covered single bed took up most of the space. Beside it, a small nightstand held a gas lamp and wind-up clock, and on the opposite wall, an oak washstand commode sat under a window. A white bowl and pitcher sat on top of the commode in front of a pair of embroidered towels that hung from the towel bar. As much as Maureen appreciated her large bedroom at home, she loved the way the small room seemed to wrap her in a warm hug.

"I regret I don't have indoor plumbing like your home," Mrs. Ambrose said. "The privy is a few steps from the back door. There's a chamber pot in the cabinet of the washstand for night-time needs. If you have things to hang, the armoire in the hall is available."

Maureen worked to hide her surprise. She hadn't ever lived in a home without indoor plumbing, not at college and not at Sophie's when she'd visited there. She'd heard many times how when her grandfather built Safe Refuge, he was one of the first in Lake Geneva to have an indoor bathroom complete with a clawfoot tub, sink, and commode in both the large home and the cottage. No wonder some of her classmates from high school used to tease her about her rich-girl life. If she did work for Pinkertons and was assigned to the frontier that was sure to change. She waved a dismissive hand. "You know I always enjoy a good adventure."

The older woman's brows rose. "I know you do, but I remember a few days there when you were so weak you had to use a bedpan. I never heard such complaining."

Maureen stared at her. "I don't remember doing that."

"I don't expect you would, given how high your fever was."

Cleaning up another person's waste had to be the most disgusting job. Having to change Doreen's diapers when she was a baby was bad enough. "Mrs. Ambrose, you've done more than I deserve. If there's anything I can do to help while I'm here, please don't hesitate to ask."

A warm smile crossed her lips. "There is only one thing I can think of."

Maureen bobbed her head. "What? Please tell me."

"Stop calling me Mrs. Ambrose. That was proper while I was your caretaker, but now I'm not, and we're friends only. My name is Beatrice, but my friends call me Bea."

Maureen grinned. "I'd love to. I hate formalities. Bea it is."

Bea returned the grin. "Good. Come sit with me in the parlor when you're ready."

After she'd hung up her few items in the armoire, and filled the washstand's bottom drawer with her underthings and night-gown, she found Bea sitting in a worn wingback chair in the parlor with her Bible open on her lap.

Bea looked up. "Oh, good you brought your Bible. That's exactly where I think we need to start our conversation." She indicated the wingback chair to her left. "Before we begin, please sit and bring me up to date on your life now that you're well."

Maureen began with the day she twisted her ankle, and how Nate's carrying her home sparked their growing attraction for each other. "Now for the difficult news. Preston, the man who sent me that letter you kept for me, came to Katie's wedding. When he caught sight of my scars he made an awful face and since then has refused to look me in the eye.

"We've been friends since we were children and recently had moved into a serious relationship. He broke up with me the day we went to the Exposition, but even so his reaction really hurt. Yesterday, I went to his home to challenge him to look at my face and not somewhere over my head. I found him drunk and belligerent. Breaking up turned out to be the best thing he has ever done for me. But now I'm confused."

Bea's eyes sparkled. "You and Nate are seeing each other now?"

She nodded. "Yes. He's wanting us to court. He even sought Da out for permission to ask me."

She pressed both palms over her heart and smiled. "Oh. That makes my heart glad. My husband and I courted before we were married. If he wants to court you, he's very serious about your relationship."

"I know. That's why I haven't given him an answer yet. I fell so hard for Preston and was certain we were to marry. I am falling in love with Nate, but if I marry him I'll never realize my dreams. Having almost died of small pox, I want to make the most of my life and not put off what's important. I told him last night about my plans to apply to Pinkerton's Detective agency to apprentice and learn how to be a detective. He says he is fine with me working and being away from home from time to time, but from his comments it's clear he is not as okay about it as he says." She blinked away the tears gathering in her eyes. "I'm so confused. Am I being selfish to want my girlhood dream over marrying the man I love?"

Bea offered a gentle smile. "I don't think your hesitation is from selfishness. You're only trying to sort things out. It wasn't hard to miss his growing affection for you taking hold over those weeks he took care of you. I used to hear him praying for you, and it touched my heart. Several times I stood just outside your door and silently prayed with him."

Maureen's heart squeezed. "He told me he prayed for me. I

think that alone showed me what a special man he is. But he said he prays for all his patients."

"Yes, he does, but not to the extent he did for you. I've never seen him spend as much time with one patient as he did with you, not only in prayer but in conversation. When he first came to see you, he'd come late morning, then have to leave to get to his afternoon appointments. It wasn't long before he came after his appointments and stayed much longer."

"I never noticed the time shift. My friends would tell me I was crazy to not agree to courtship and marriage and would regret it later."

"It sounds to me you are also asking yourself if you choose your detective dream over being with Nate would you later regret the decision."

If she had half as much intuitiveness as Bea, she'd be happy. "You're right. That's crossed my mind more than once. He says he fell for me before I became ill when I sold him a dresser at the furniture store where I worked before I caught smallpox. I felt some attraction to him then, but I was over the moon for Preston and blamed it on his good looks and easygoing manner. Now here I am in a quagmire I can't seem to shake. If I really loved him, wouldn't I willingly give up my dreams to be with him?"

"Not necessarily. You've had that dream for years and you've only known Nate a short time. But you're leaving one element out of all of this."

Maureen frowned. "What?"

"If it's God's will that you and Nate continue falling in love and marry, then that is why he became attracted to you that day in the furniture store. I understand your doubting Nate's feelings, but I can assure you the man is entirely smitten with you in a way that has nothing to do with your having been his patient. But aside from that, I watched him care for you through those weeks. Many times, it was me applying cold cloths to your forehead, but often it was Nate.

"Sometimes while I was washing your dirty linens or preparing a meal for you, it was he who tended to you making sure you were as comfortable as possible. Even though he is vaccinated, he wore a mask as a precaution because some people have caught smallpox even after getting the shot. It was still a risk. God has protected many of our physicians through this epidemic and he protected Nate for sure.

Tears pricked at Maureen's eyes "I had no idea."

Bea lifted a lid on a small basket sitting on a table between their chairs and plucked out a handkerchief. She handed it to Maureen. "I put in a supply for times like this. Feel free to use them anytime."

Maureen thanked her and dabbed her eyes. "Lately I've been like a never-ending fountain. You'd think I'd have run out of tears by now."

"There's a verse that says God stores up all our tears in a bottle. Perhaps that's how they can be restored so fast."

Maureen flipped the pages of her Bible. "Where is that found?"

Bea turned a few pages in her own Bible. Here it is. Psalm 56:8. Thou tellest my wanderings: put thou my tears into thy bottle: are they not in thy book?

"God knows every minute of our sufferings, and He collects all our tears for the day when there will be no more crying or pain. Then He'll take that bottle and toss it into the sea." She smiled. "That's the Bea Ambrose translation. I like to extend my thoughts that are started by a verse."

Maureen dabbed her eyes. "I like your translation and the picture of all my suffering being tossed away by God. Regarding my feelings for Nate, it's easier to love a person who accepts you as you are than to love one who can't bear to look at your deformities. I only want to be sure my feelings for him will grow with time into the same kind of love my parents share.

"I'm sensing God is redirecting me through this. My mother is appalled at my dream of being a private detective, but ever since I heard of Kate Warne, a lady Pinkerton detective who helped protect Lincoln from an assassination attempt, I've wanted to follow in her footsteps. Now I'm realizing that maybe God wants me helping others in a different way." She looked Bea in the eyes. "I want to be you."

CHAPTER TWENTY-SIX

Maureen averted her gaze from the shocked expression on Bea's face. Where did those words come from? The thought wasn't exactly foreign, but it was the first time she'd put it into words. Would Bea think she was weird? She brought her gaze back to the older woman and startled. "Oh, Bea, I didn't mean to make you cry. I'm sure I must sound daft. I mean I want to live my life as a reflection of your compassion and commitment to the Lord. Not the way I've been living up to now."

Bea dabbed at her eyes with a handkerchief. "Child, I'm not crying because you've hurt me, and I certainly don't think you are daft. I'm honored and touched. My prayer almost daily is that I live my life before younger women as a pattern of how to live in reverence to the Lord. I'm glad you are thinking about all these things and not making decisions on emotion only."

Maureen wiped the tears rolling down her cheeks with her hanky. Why did the truth have to hurt so much? It wasn't like she hadn't already thought about how Preston's emotional condition had awakened her to her misguided understanding of her feelings for him. "I've not appreciated how my parents have tried to redirect me when my spirited desire for adventure pulls me away from what they've often said. We need to honor God first along with the Bible and seek to do His will above our own. I was too busy going after what I wanted to pay attention.

"You remind me of a young horse my husband and I once owned. Albert could break most any mustang or colt that came his way. But one beautiful chestnut refused to be mastered. Once, he bucked Albert off so hard he broke his arm."

Maureen gasped. "I hope I'm not that bad."

"Oh, no. The comparison stops with refusing to let anyone master you except yourself. What that little horse couldn't understand is that we all have a Master greater than us, and when we surrender to Him, it's not giving up and being under an evil dictator, but surrendering to His loving care and provision. Knowing that no matter what happens—good or bad—He's in control and we can trust in Him."

Maureen flipped to the psalm Bea had read and scanned the verse, then read the psalm in its entirety. Her friend made sense. God could have allowed her suffering to break her determination to live her life her way and let Him show her His will. Still there was a slight nudge within to resist. Was her desire for independence so strong she couldn't change?

She looked at Bea. "I want to surrender to the Lord, but a part of me wants to resist."

Bea slid onto her knees on the floor. "Come down here and join me. There's nothing like praying on your knees to humble one's self."

When she was little, she used to kneel by her bed to say her bedtime prayers with either Mama or Da saying them with her. It was time she started again. She slid to her knees.

"Come closer so we can hold hands."

She scooted closer and took Bea's hand, noticing the calluses from a long life of hard work. "I don't know how to begin."

"Yes, you do. How do you usually start your prayers?"

She didn't want to admit that recently she only said little prayers in her mind at the time of need. "I don't pray long prayers. Just short ones like 'God help me.' It's been a while since I've prayed long prayers on my own."

Bea studied her. "I heard you praying when you were sick. Longish prayers sometimes."

"I did?"

"Yes. I presumed that was how you always prayed. Young lady, whether you realize it or not, prayer is going on deep in your soul. Maybe later when you're alone it will come easier. I'll begin."

Maureen chose not to vocally add to Bea's prayer and prayed silently in her heart as Bea asked for God to give Maureen courage and wisdom and a heart of compassion to be used the way God wanted it to be used.

After Bea said, "Amen," she looked at Maureen. "I think you should come with me to a job I was just notified about. When they called this morning, I told them I'd have to let them know because I have a houseguest. It's only for tomorrow while the regular caretaker takes a day off. A young girl on a farm the other side of Delavan has smallpox. She's struggling with the scars she knows are to come and I think encouragement from someone other than an old lady like me can work wonders."

Maureen gaped at her. "Am I qualified?"

You are one hundred percent qualified, and your faith is strong. You said you want to help others, especially those who are suffering with the same disease. A day with me and this young girl will give you a taste of what it's like to care for the seriously ill."

Maureen pushed back the desire to decline. It was only for one day, and what if she could help the girl? "Okay. I'll do it,"

THE FOLLOWING MORNING, Maureen climbed into the back of the wagon owned by the sick girl's father. Bea sat beside her and spread a wool blanket over the two of them.

Mr. Duncan, the girl's father, glanced over his shoulder. "We're most obliged you could come on short notice, Mrs. Ambrose. I know Laura will be pleased to have you taking care of her."

"It's my pleasure. How is she doing?"

"I'm told the scabs look like they are about to come off. The doctor says she's through the worst of it. But she's really down. Can't say I blame her."

"Hopefully my friend here will be able to help. Maureen recently went through the same thing."

He focused on Maureen and nodded. "I'm sorry to interrupt your visit. We really appreciate your helping today."

Maureen tugged the blanket up around her chin to stop her teeth from chattering. "Like Bea—Mrs. Ambrose—said, it's my pleasure."

When they arrived at the Duncan's farm, Mr. Duncan placed a medical mask on his face, then took them around to the back of the house and knocked on a closed door that had a quarantine sign affixed to it.

A voice that sounded like that belonging to a young girl beckoned them in, and Mr. Duncan opened the door partway and stuck his head through. "Laura, Mrs. Ambrose is here. She's brought someone you might like to meet. They've both had smallpox and don't need to wear masks." He opened the door wider and stepped aside so the woman could enter. "The privy is outside the back door. I'll be in the barn if you need anything. My wife is taking our son to school and will be back soon."

Maureen followed Bea into what appeared to be a sunroom in normal times. The makeshift sickroom had been made quite comfortable with a bed, dresser and washstand commode. Already, Maureen mentally prayed her thanks to God that she had indoor plumbing available to her during her illness. A puffy quilt covered the bed with the only evidence of a person beneath it a pink night cap.

Bea approached the bed and bent down. "Laura, I'm Mrs. Ambrose and like your father said, I've brought a friend. Maureen recently had smallpox."

A pair of hands emerged from beneath the quilt and pushed the covering away from the girl's face.

At the sight of multiple scabs covering her face, Maureen's heart squeezed. She stepped next to Bea and looked into a pair of frightened eyes. "Hi, Laura. I know exactly how you feel. I used to have visions in my head how I'd look when all the scabs fell off. But you know what? Not every scab means a scar. A lot of them do. I had some on my face but look at me. One side has scars but the other side doesn't.

Laura scooted up and Bea arranged another pillow behind the girl's back. She studied Maureen's face then raised her hand as if she were going to touch Maureen's cheek, but paused.

Maureen took Laura's hand and placed it on her left cheek. "Already the scars have lessened. They'll never completely go away. It was hard at first. I even wore a scarf over them for my sister's wedding. Of course, everyone saw the scars whenever the breeze lifted the fabric, but I felt better anyway. Now I like to call them my battle scars. We're special people. Lots of people have unseen battle scars deep inside where they've been hurt by someone's words or actions. Our scars are visible, and mine remind me of how far God has brought me.

Tears gathered in Laura's eyes and Maureen wrapped her arms around her. After they separated, Laura said. "It feels so good to hug someone. Thank you. I need to sleep right now."

While Laura slept, Bea and Maureen made tea in the home's kitchen, then Bea carried their steaming cups to a sitting area at the far end of the sun porch. Maureen sipped her tea before setting the cup on the table and lowering her voice. "I've been praying about something while you were heating up the water."

"Care to share?"

She shook her head. "Later. I'm not ready yet to discuss it. It's too new."

By the time Laura's father brought them back to Bea's, the sun was low on the horizon. Although the air was chilly, Maureen didn't feel cold at all. She'd thoroughly enjoyed the day helping with Laura and was glad she still had tomorrow with Bea, because she had one more thing to discuss.

CHAPTER TWENTY-SEVEN

The next morning, Maureen woke before dawn and lay there praying and thanking God for his gift of yesterday with Laura. For the first time, she had clarity of mind and was certain God was showing her He had a better way for her to still have adventure in her life. She couldn't wait to talk to Nate. If he cared for her as much as Bea claimed, he needed to know what she was considering. She'd contact Da to come for her after work tonight, or, at the very least, early tomorrow.

An hour later, she climbed out of the warm bed and washed her face. She paused her hand and ran her fingertips over the scars on her left cheek then did the same over the smooth skin on her right cheek. One short month ago, she couldn't have done that. Now, she praised God for the scars, feeling like she'd earned every one of them.

Wearing a shirtwaist and skirt, she made her way down the short hall to the parlor, expecting to have some time alone in the Bible before Bea was up. She stepped into the room and chuckled. "I should have known you'd be awake already. Here I've been tiptoeing around."

"Ha. I don't think I've slept past five in my whole life. Good morning. Once you've had your breakfast, we can discuss whatever is on your heart. I sense you've grown a lot since yesterday and may not need much more talk from me."

Maureen crossed the room and patted the woman on her shoulder. "I think I will always need more talk from you. You have a knack of straightening out all the kinks in my brain."

After Maureen had eaten a bran muffin Bea had made earlier and prepared a second cup of tea, she settled in the same chair as yesterday and opened her Bible. "Last night I read Psalm 139 before I went to sleep and was struck where it says all the days of my life were written before one of them has happened. It helps to see that God knew beforehand I would be sick but survive. He could have prevented these scars, or he could have not allowed me to live. I need to be willing to let him lead me in new directions. I'm thinking of becoming a nurse."

Bea clapped her hands and grinned. "That very thought came to me as I watched you yesterday talking to Laura and later giving her a sponge bath. I prayed if that thought was from God that He would show it to be true."

Maureen was sure her grin was going to break her face if it stretched any wider. "I'll need to find a good nursing school." She glanced down at the Bible. "I don't know how Nate fits into my life or even if he wants to fit in anymore after our last discussion."

"The only way you'll know how he feels is to talk to him, but there's nothing wrong with taking it slow for a while."

A loud ring broke through the air and Maureen jumped. "I still can't get used to hearing a telephone."

Bea scurried to the kitchen. "I'm hoping someday they can make it a little softer. I may be old, but I'm not hard of hearing." A minute later she returned. "It's Nate for you. Do you suppose his ears were ringing just now? After all, we were talking about him."

Maureen smiled. "I always thought that was an old myth, but

maybe there's some truth in it." She went to the telephone and put the earpiece to her ear. "Hi Nate."

"Good morning. I have some bad news. Preston is very ill. It seems after your altercation the other day, he continued to drink all that day and into yesterday. He's developed alcohol poisoning. He could die if he's not watched at all times to be sure he doesn't fall asleep or become nauseated. He's asking for you."

A sinking feeling came over her. Had she made Pres worse by confronting him? If she hadn't gone over there he'd probably have slept off the booze from overnight and not drunk anymore the rest of the day.

"Mo, are you still there?"

She pressed her fingertips to her right temple and pressed. "Yes. Do you think it's wise for me to go to him? If he started drinking more after I left him—"

"He would have gotten to this point if not today, then another day. You can't blame yourself for this. I think it might help if you'd come and see him for a few minutes."

Hadn't she just told Bea she wanted to be like her? Bea would already have her coat on and been on her way. "Of course, I'll come. I'll call my father and see if he can get away."

"No need to bother him. I'll come for you. I have a nurse staying with Preston, and his parents are here. They're all making sure he stays hydrated and doesn't fall asleep. I can be there within the hour."

"I'll be ready."

After telling Bea what happened, the women prayed for Preston to recover and that he'd be able to get his life straightened around. They also prayed for Maureen to say the right words when she saw him. By the time Nate pulled his carriage into the drive, she was packed and waiting.

She opened the front door before he reached the porch. Seeing him standing there, his beard neatly trimmed and his blue eyes twinkling as they always did when she saw him, her pulse raced. She resisted the urge to fall into his arms. *That can come later.* "Hi, Nate. I'm ready to go."

He ran his gaze over her frame and pulled her into a side hug. "It's good to see you. I'll say hello to Bea, then get your bag."

After a short goodbye, she and Nate returned to his carriage and he got the horse moving toward Lake Geneva. They'd traveled a few minutes down the state road, when he placed his hand over hers and squeezed it. "You may have been gone only two days, but I missed you."

She returned the squeeze. "I missed you too, Nate, but the time was so needed. God taught me a lot. I hope you have time to talk later."

"I cleared my schedule to be available to Preston. If he's doing okay and hasn't regressed, we can take a walk down by the lake later."

The ride passed quickly as he recounted his past couple of days, taking care of a patient who was soon to deliver a baby, and then yesterday being called by Preston's father saying Pres hadn't answered the telephone for the past couple of days. The boat company said they'd let him go because they caught him drinking on the job.

He glanced over at Maureen. "As best I can figure out, that happened the night before you went over there."

She mulled that over. "So, losing the job is what triggered the binge, but I certainly didn't help with my visit. I presume after Mr. Stevens's call you went right over to Shelter Bay."

"Yes. I found him almost completely passed out and incoherent lying on the parlor floor in a pool of vomit. I got the mess cleaned up and helped him to bed, then immediately called in a nurse to stay with him. Preston's parents made immediate plans to come to the lake.

As they turned up South Shore Drive toward Shelter Bay,

she glanced at him. "Was there something I could have done to help him not turn to alcohol?"

He put both reins in his left hand and drew her to his side with his other arm. "My sweet Maureen, his pain isn't from you. It's the deep pain he's been fighting ever since he failed to save that boy during the storm. His state of mind is something the medical community is just now starting to learn about. Men who came out of the Civil War battles have displayed behaviors similar to Preston's. It's referred to as "shell shock.""

She digested his words. "Preston mentioned it was like shell shock. But he wasn't in a war battle."

"Apparently, it can be triggered by more than artillery sounds. It's something I need to learn more about. People start to drink a lot when their emotional pain is excessive. That much I know. Alcohol is like a quadruple dose of Laudanum for him."

"I feel so bad no one could help him."

He leaned over and kissed her damp cheek and whispered in her ear. "I love your compassion for others."

Wasn't that what she just told Mrs. Ambrose she wanted? A warm feeling washed over her, and she silently thanked God for putting Nate in her life. She rested her head on his shoulder, loving being back in his presence after a two-day absence.

Soon, he guided the carriage into the Shelter Bay drive, and they came to a stop next to the hitching post. In a way, the large home had been a shelter for Preston. In this case, too much of one. Being continuously alone for the past couple of months, alcohol must have been like a friend to him. If she became a nurse, she wanted to learn as much as she could about the cause of Preston's condition and how to work with its victims.

Horace Stevens stepped through the back door, his clothing rumpled and his eyes framed by dark circles. He approached the carriage and assisted Maureen from her seat. "Thanks for coming, Maureen."

She nodded. "It's the least I can do. I hope it helps."

Nate climbed out and came around to where they stood. "Any changes since I left, Horace?"

"No. He tries to sleep, but as soon as one of us shakes him he comes awake, madder than anything at being woke up. He almost caught me on the jaw last time." He faced Maureen and drew her into a side hug. "How are you, Maureen? Not the most pleasant reason for us to be together again."

"I'm doing much better since you last saw me. My ankle is healed up, and I'm ready to rejoin the world. But enough about me. It's Preston I'm concerned about. Is it okay to see him now?"

Mr. Stevens nodded. "Yes. He's been waiting for you, but I need to warn you. He's not himself."

Nate stepped forward. "Let's go up if you're ready, Maureen."

"As ready as I'll ever be. Lead the way." As they entered the home's back hall. Mrs. Stevens stepped out of a door on the left that led to the kitchen, a tea cup in hand. "Maureen, thank you for coming. Would you like some tea before you go up?"

She shook her head. "No, thank you. I had plenty before Nate came for me. I was with a friend in Delavan."

"As I understand. All the more reason to thank you for cutting your visit short. I just got off the telephone with your mother. They know to expect you later."

Nate came up beside her. "I'll take you up now."

She let him take her hand, and he led her to the staircase. Upstairs, they walked to a half-open door and he faced her. "Wait here a moment while I check on things."

She nodded, grateful for another few minutes to collect herself. Nate's words earlier helped to lessen the inclination to blame herself, but a part of her still did. She hated that the last words spoken between them were ugly and accusing. It seemed so important at the time to get him to accept her scarred face. Now it mattered not at all.

Nate returned, worry lines creasing his brow. "There's basically been no change, but he's ready to see you."

They stepped into the room. With sunshine spilling in through the window and the electric lights turned on it was a wonder he could sleep it was so bright, yet his eyes were closed. A woman wearing a nurse uniform shook his arm. "Preston wake up"

He lifted his left hand and swatted her away as if she were a fly. "No."

Nate approached the bed. "Preston, Maureen is here."

Pres's eyes popped open. "Where is she?" The raspy voice, so low she struggled to discern the words, startled her.

"I'm here, Pres." She moved closer and at the stench of whisky swallowed back a gag. Drawing in a deep breath, she stepped to Nate's side and worked hard to not gasp at Pres's once muscular arms now almost too thin. Normally he would have asked for a long-sleeved shirt to wear over his knit short-sleeved undershirt while she was there, but he'd apparently gone beyond caring about his appearance. She swallowed back a sob and lifted his left hand from where it rested at his side and squeezed. "Pres, I'm so sorry you're ill."

His hand stayed limp in her grasp. "I'm not sick that way, Mo. I did this to myself. I hate to have you see me like this."

"Preston—"

"Don't feel sorry for me, Mo. I've made my peace with God and my life is in His hands. If he wills me to get through this and I live, I intend to make something of my life before it's over. I can't do that unless I make peace with you."

She squeezed his hand again. "Preston, save your energy. There's always been peace between us."

"I hurt your feelings by not accepting you with your scars, and that was wrong. You are a sweet, wonderful woman. It's what's inside that counts."

She opened her mouth, but no words came out.

"Are you going after that detective job?"

"Smallpox changed me, Pres. God has shown me I need to do His will and stop seeking only my own interests. I have something in mind that might surprise you, but I'll wait until another time to share it.'

The corners of his mouth lifted into a slight smile. "That's great, but you haven't said you forgive me for how I hurt you and acting like a dolt at the wedding. I also want forgiveness for taking you to the fair where you probably caught smallpox."

Her throat tightened. Never had she thought that for one second. "I already forgave you for what you said that day. As for my catching smallpox being your fault, I could have caught it anywhere. Even right here in Lake Geneva. I fully believe God allowed it to show me truths I would never have learned otherwise. There's more to life than good looks. Like the proverb says, Beauty is passing but the woman who fears the Lord should be praised. And I might add looking out only for your own interests is not what God wants from any of us. I don't hold you responsible for taking me to the fair."

The worry lines that had creased the paper-thin skin around his eyes dissolved. "Thank you. And thanks for coming. Did Nate bring you?"

"Yes. I was in Delavan visiting the woman who took care of me when I was sick."

"Nate's a good man for you, Maureen. Don't mess things up."

"I don't intend to." She bent and placed a gentle kiss on his forehead. "Until we meet again."

She straightened and faced Nate. "I need some air."

Nate turned to the nurse. "I'll be back in about an hour. If there's a need for me earlier, you can reach me at Safe Refuge."

THAT EVENING, snuggled in her winter coat, Maureen gripped Nate's hand as they strolled down the shore path near Safe Refuge. She looked up at him. "How did things go with Preston after you got back?"

"Good news. He's turned the corner, and you are to thank for that. For the first time, he showed an interest in bathing and putting on clean clothes. His mother immediately went about filling the tub in the bathroom with soapy water, and he was able to take his own bath without assistance. He then put on a clean work shirt and dungarees. He still needs to stay awake, but I don't think it will be much longer before we're sure the alcohol is totally out of his system."

"That's wonderful news, but I didn't do anything except hold his hand and talk to him. How can I have been a help?"

"You assured him he was forgiven. It could have gone either way after that. Sometimes the person feels relieved that he can now die in peace or be inspired to get better."

"I took a bath too. I felt grimy and stinky after being there."

"Trust me. You didn't stink at all."

"You were probably used to the smell having been with him all that time."

"Possibly. Did you mean what you said to Preston when he said to not mess things up with me?"

She was grateful it was too dark for him to see the smile on her face. "What did I say, I can't remember."

"Don't give me that. You remember." He gave her hand a squeeze.

A giggle burst from her throat. "No, I don't."

He stopped and pulled her into a hug. "Sure, you do."

"No, I don't."

He kissed her. "You said you don't intend to."

"Intend to do what?"

"Mess things up with me."

"That's right. I did say that. I think this is a good time to share about my time with Bea."

They joined hands again and continue to walk. "I'm guessing what you're about to tell me is related to what you said to Preston?"

"You'll see. My time with Bea was priceless, Nate. She showed me scriptures that helped me understand about God's will and how He has a purpose for everything that happens in my life. That includes getting smallpox and meeting you and what happens in my future.

"I hope meeting me isn't lumped in the same category as smallpox."

She laughed. "Not directly, but I had no idea you were there as much as you were when I was at my worst. She said she heard you praying over me several times and that touched me a lot."

"As you worsened I prayed harder than ever because, as I've said before, you were more than a patient to me." He stopped walking and embraced her. "You are very precious to me, Mo. I didn't want to lose you." He bent down and kissed her.

They parted and continued down the path hand in hand. "Pres was right. Nate was a good man. Da had all but said the same thing. But until she discussed nursing school with him, she couldn't say what she felt. "What you said warms my heart more than you know. A couple of days ago, Bea received a last-minute call to take care of a young girl with smallpox there in Delavan, and I went along with her. Laura was fifteen years old and had a lot of scabs forming all over her face. Of course, Laura was devastated.

"While I gave her a sponge bath, I talked about my own feelings and experience, mentioning some things Bea had talked to me about the night before. Laura, Bea, and I prayed together, and the three of us decided we are wearing our battle scars and are ready to face the world. I promised to visit her again soon and went home with Bea, feeling on top of the world."

He let go of her hand and circled her waist with his arm and tugged her to his side. "Battle scars. What a wonderful way to view them. I may borrow that with my patients when such things come up."

A warm feeling came over her. "I'd be honored."

"It's a marvelous perspective, and one that I sense came from God. Do you have any more words of wisdom?"

"I don't know if it's words of wisdom, but while I was caring for Laura yesterday a strong sense came over me that I should think about becoming a nurse. I didn't attribute it to anything except my enjoyment of being able to help someone who is suffering how I have suffered. But this morning when I shared the idea with Bea, she said she had the same idea come to her while I was bathing Laura. Bea said the Holy Spirit was working within both of us at the same time. I plan to start looking for a good nursing school and maybe begin classes as early as January."

"Oh Maureen, I'm excited for you." He hugged her. "While you were having your epiphany, I was making a commitment to God to love you enough to let you go and do whatever you desire. I'll be happy to help you find a good nursing school."

"You know that might mean my leaving Lake Geneva for at least a year."

He kissed her. "Do you think I'm going to suggest anything farther away than a couple hour's train ride? Schools usually don't meet on weekends."

"Oh Nate. I was afraid when I told you my plans, you'd want to stop seeing me."

"On the contrary, with you becoming a nurse, there's no telling what God might have in store for the both of us"

CHAPTER TWENTY-EIGHT

*P*reston stood on Shelter Bay's dock and stared out at
the water. Because of November's mild tempera-
tures many lakeshore estates were just now taking down their
piers for the winter. Dad and his brothers were expected in a
couple of days to get the *Ida* in drydock. He wanted to help, but
unless he could put on waders and stand in the chilly water
without a panic attack he'd be of no use.

He'd been standing on the pier for ten minutes. At about the
seven-minute mark, his pulse had increased, at eight minutes,
his fingers tingled, and now, he couldn't take in a deep breath.
He wanted to run for the shore and get away, but his will was
stronger. He wasn't moving. He'd overcome his alcohol craving
—been dry a week already—and he'd overcome this too. His
mother had stayed by his side through the whole ugly with-
drawal, and was the only one still with him now. The nurse
Nate Murphy had assigned to Preston came daily to check on
him, but Murphy hadn't been there for several days.

He turned and glanced up the hill. Mom stood on the patio,
arms crossed, eyes on him as if he might have a stash on the

"

pier. Didn't she realize that having gone through the shakes, the headaches, and the fever that finally broke yesterday he never wanted to be in that state again?

Off to the northwest, dark clouds had started to build. So much like that fateful day last August. But this was Geneva Lake. No schooners plied these waters, and this was November. That kind of storm didn't happen in late autumn. A little rain and thunder wasn't going to make him move. He scanned the lake's choppy surface as flashes of lightning sliced through the approaching charcoal-colored clouds. Warnings were likely issued for all craft to stay off the lake until the storm passed over. Standard procedure.

A gust slapped him in the face and he gripped a piling as the angry wind pushed against him. He'd stay as long as he could stand it. He had to get rid of this fear. Along the shore, trees bent nearly to the ground and he gripped the piling with both hands.

Waves higher than his almost six feet slammed against the shore and the *Ida* bounced with the rise and fall of the lake chop. She slammed into the dock and the sound of breaking glass rose on the wind. He winced. Someone must have left something unsecured in the cabin.

Without warning, the steam yacht *Celerity* careened past him, not more than fifteen feet from the end of the pier. Its captain frantically worked the wheel to keep the vessel traveling with the waves and not against them. A moment ago, he'd seen nothing on the water. He waved at the captain, but with the shroud of darkness suddenly thrust on them he didn't seem to notice Preston. The boat suddenly changed course and headed away from the shoreline and into the waves. Where was the man going?

Preston glanced up at the house. The rain was coming like sheets and he barely made out his mother watching from one of the large parlor windows. She knew it was unsafe to stand in front of a window in such a wind, but she was worried for him.

He turned back and searched through the pounding rain for the *Celerity*. He spotted her in the middle of the lake tossing about like a child's toy. *Please Lord let them get through this squall.*

A jagged bolt of lightning split the sky, illuminating the vessel's bow as it disappeared into the water. He counted off the seconds while he waited for the steamboat to pop up. After reaching ten with no sight of her, he pulled off his shoes. How many people besides the captain were on board?

The darkest part of the sky had moved west and was as far down as Fontana. The waters nearby calmed as several cushions floated on the surface. Preston worked his shoes off and shed his jacket. He tossed it on the dock, then dove in. The bite of the cold water took his breath away, but he ignored it and swam toward the cushions where they marked the site of the boat's sinking. He dove. There were people on that boat. It wasn't too late. Bits of debris—a man's hat, a woman's purse, a shoe— floated around him, obstructing his view. Memories of his looking for the boy and groping in the water flashed through his mind. He couldn't let it happen again.

A woman drifted upward as she passed him. He kicked to the water's surface and sucked in a lungful of air as he scanned the water. Her body floated a few feet away, kept afloat by what looked like inflated blue balloons. He swam toward her. The "balloons" weren't balloons at all but were her dress's large sleeves. After verifying she had a pulse, he kept hold of her as he started for Shelter Bay's pier, thankful for the calm waters.

He reached the dock and lifted the woman toward his mother who had come from the house. "Put your arms under hers and pull her gently onto the dock then place her on her stomach."

After his mom did as he asked, he scrambled up the ladder

and arranged the woman's arms to the correct position. He then knelt in front of her head, pressed his palms to her back, raised her elbows and let them down, and repeated the process. He glanced at his mother. "Mom, can you check for her pulse?"

Mom pressed two fingers against the woman's wrist. "She has one but it's not strong."

He continued forcing the respirations another couple of minutes. The woman coughed and spit up water. "That's what I wanted to see." He turned the woman over and gently shook her by her shoulders. "Please wake up. Tell me who you are."

Her eyes fluttered open, and she stared at Preston and tried to sit up.

Using gentle pressure, Preston pressed his palm on one of her shoulders. "Best you lie here a few minutes."

She focused on him, her eyes full of fear. "Who are you and where am I?"

I'm Preston Stevens, you were in a boat that capsized in a storm. I just pulled you out of the water. What is your name?"

"Margaret Spencer." She rose up on an elbow. "My mother and aunt were with me on the boat."

Preston scanned the lake. Several boats circled where the *Celerity* went down. He didn't have the heart to tell her he saw no other survivors. He rested his hand on her shoulder. "I've served in the U.S. Life Saving Service and you're safe. We're on my family's pier. Please remain still until I've assessed you."

His mother stepped over. "I'm Ida Stevens, this young man's mother." She held out a blanket. "She's shivering, Pres. Can she be covered?"

"One second." He quickly checked for broken bones. Not finding any, he helped her sit up and his mother wrapped the blanket over her shoulders. He looked off down the lake toward town. "Looks like help is on the way." He stood and waved as the *Admiral,* one of the vessels owned by his former employer, honked and came toward them.

He looked at his mother. "Where did that blanket come from?"

"I brought it with me when I saw you dive in the water."

The *Admiral* came alongside the dock and Bill O'Grady, the boat's captain, tossed a rope to Preston. He wrapped it around a cleat. "Bill, this is Margaret Spencer. She needs medical attention."

Bill stepped onto the dock. "Good to see you again, Preston. Good job."

Preston shrugged. "Not very heroic. It was her puffy sleeves that kept her afloat."

"If you hadn't been there to bring her in, she wouldn't likely have survived."

"I agree. He's my hero." Margaret looked out toward the lake. "Where are the others? My aunt and mother were with me."

"I'm not sure," Bill said. "They may be at other piers. Let's get you to Doctor Murphy. I'll check around and see if your family is being tended to."

Together they got Margaret onto the *Admiral* and Preston laid out several cushions on the deck as a makeshift bed. He and Bill helped her lie down. Bill covered her with a dry blanket from the boat's supply and handed the damp blanket to Nate. "I believe this is yours."

Preston patted Margaret on her shoulder. "You're in good hands now." He jumped back over to the dock and Bill got the boat headed for town.

His mom rubbed his back and handed him his discarded jacket. "Put this on. You're shivering."

He slipped his arms in the jacket sleeves, then worked into his shoes and started down the dock toward the house.

Mom walked along side of him. "I'm proud of you, son."

"It's what I was trained to do, Mom. But I couldn't have done it without your help. We made a good team."

"It was all you. I only followed your directions. I wouldn't be surprised if you're rewarded for what you did."

"My reward is that I think my fear is gone, but time will tell. I wish there were more survivors. I fear she's the only one."

CHAPTER TWENTY-NINE

$\mathcal{M}$aureen sat at the big house's kitchen table, pouring over material Nate had given her about nursing schools. She'd narrowed her choice down to one in Milwaukee and one in Evanston, Illinois.

The Evanston school held the most promise because of its proximity to her Aunt Callie's home, where she could stay during the week and easily take the train home on weekends. Distance and time apart were not good for a romantic relationship. Nate had already told her he would help her with her studies and she could assist him in the office on Saturdays. She was already dreaming of working alongside him after she graduated in a year.

The backdoor bells jangled, and she glanced at the clock. Had Nate come by during his lunch break? Grinning, she walked to the door and opened it. The grin dissolved. "Preston. Hello."

He stared at his feet then raised his head. "Hi, Mo. I decided it was better to come in person rather than use the telephone." He glanced over her shoulder. "Are you alone?"

"If you mean is Nate here? He's working. Mama is here. I

think she's upstairs." She opened the door wider. At least he seemed clear headed. "It's good to see you sober and looking a lot better than when I last saw you. Come in." She stepped back, and he entered the hall. She had to admit he looked the best he had in a long time. Fresh haircut, scruff shaved from his face, coat and tie, polished boots. "I was in the kitchen going over materials about nursing schools. We can sit there."

His brows rose. "Nursing school? What happened to being a detective?"

"I've changed in many ways since being sick."

They entered the kitchen and she walked to the table and gathered up the papers strewn across the table, arranging them into a neat pile. "Please sit. I was about to make a cup of tea. Would you like some?"

He held up a hand. "Nothing for me. Go ahead and fix yours."

"I can wait." She sat.

He took a chair to her right. "I've been clean for almost two weeks, thanks to you. I might be dead by now if you hadn't come over that day."

She waved a hand. "You give me too much credit. You supplied the determination."

He laid a newspaper on the table. "Have you seen this?"

She shook her head. "Da usually brings it home later in the afternoon. Why?"

"Then you probably haven't heard what happened during last week's freak storm."

She shook her head. "I've been too consumed with my future plans and helping Da a bit in the greenhouse." *And spending time with Nate.*

"When the storm came up, I decided to force myself to stay on the pier to work through my fear. The *Celerity* suddenly appeared and came so close I was sure it was going to crash into our dock, but it made a turn and headed back out. The lightning was ferocious and lit up the whole lake. The *Celerity* was being tossed around, and I felt so helpless watching her. Then she went under." He paused to swallow.

"Oh Pres, how horrible. As I recall, the storm was over almost as fast as it began."

"After the worst was over, all I saw of the boat was cushions floating around. I saw no people." He went on to tell how he dove in and swam to where the boat went down. "A woman floated past me. Her sleeves were like yours but bigger and they filled with air. That's what kept her afloat."

"They're called mutton sleeves. I never thought of them as life saving devices, but I see how that could happen. Was she alive?"

"Barely. I got her to the pier and my mother helped me get her onto the dock where I started artificial respiration. She's fine now. The entire story is in this week's paper. The good news is I've no more fear of the water. I'm almost my old self again, and because of what I did, I've been hired back by the boat company as an assistant to the captain on the *Admiral*."

"Pres, that's wonderful news. I remember Nate saying he treated the only survivor of that boat accident. You were there at the right time. I'm so proud of you." She leaned over and gave him a side hug.

His arms circled around her waist and he tugged her closer. She tried to wriggle away, but he resisted, almost causing her chair to tip over. He continued to hold her tight against him. "Maureen I'm so sorry for how I treated you. I still love you." He brought his mouth to hers and kissed her hard.

She managed to slide her hands between them and pressed her palms against his chest, but he hugged her tighter, then kissed her hard again. His hands slid down her back and he pushed his fingers against her waistband. She twisted away from him and stood, then pointed toward the door. "Get out right now."

He leaned back and looked up at her "I'm sorry, Mo. I never intended to go that far."

She smoothed her blouse. "Please leave now!"

His face fell and he stared at his lap. "I know better, please hear me out. We've always said since we were kids that one day we'd marry and see the world together. I was hoping we could start over by eloping and heading to New York. We can book passage on one of those freighters that also take on a few passengers. Along the way I can pick up a job here and there to save money for the next stop. It would be our dream trip,"

She shook her head. "I've fallen in love with someone else, Preston."

"But we've always loved each other. You can't love Murphy like you love me."

"You're right I don't love him the same. I love him in a lasting way that ours never did. It's over, Preston. We're through."

A grimace took over his features, then dissolved into no expression at all. She braced herself to scream if what she said triggered another aggressive move.

He scraped his chair back, stood, and squared his shoulders. He leveled his eyes on her. "If you change your mind, call me. We can be gone in a month." He turned on his heel and left the kitchen. A few moments later, the door to the outside slammed.

Maureen sat in silence, shaking so hard her teeth chattered.

"Did I hear a man's voice? Was Nate here?" Mama stepped into the kitchen.

Should she tell her what happened or let it go? "It was Preston, wanting to win me back. Did you know that he saved a woman during that terrible storm last week?" She pushed the newspaper across the table. "The article is in here. He said it snapped him out of his fear of the water. He's quit drinking and wants me to elope with him on a worldwide jaunt, stopping here and there to earn money along the way."

Mama's brows rose. "Doesn't he know you are in a serious relationship with Nate?"

"Yes, but he was hoping my spirit for adventure would overcome that."

Her mother picked up the newspaper and opened it. "Local Man to Be Honored as a Hero. Rather impressive headline." She read for a few moments. "It says here the town is planning to award him a citation for his heroism."

Maureen's eyes widened. "I didn't read it. He told me how it happened but never mentioned being honored. Although he did say the boat company offered him a new job as an assistant to the captain of the *Admiral*."

Mama pointed to the papers Maureen had been working on. "Did you tell him you're planning on nursing school?"

"Of course, and I told him I was in love with someone else, but it was like he didn't hear me. One good thing. I'm no longer confused about my calling regarding nursing school or my future husband." She gathered the papers from the table. "Of course, Nate hasn't proposed as yet, so the marriage part of my calling may not happen. I feel the need to be by myself for a while. I'll be in the cottage."

Her mother smiled. "You know good and well he's going to propose soon. The man is head over heels in love with you. It's written all over his face whenever he's with you."

"I hope you're right." She headed for the door. She probably should have told Mama how aggressive Pres became. His fear may have been cured but his impulsive behavior was still there.

As she started across the flagstone path to the cottage the sound of horse hooves intruded and she turned.

Nate waved and she waited for him to halt the carriage and climb down. He came across the grass and bent to kiss her cheek, then handed her a folded newspaper. "I thought you'd like to see the main story on the front page. I had no idea when I treated the woman who almost drowned that it was Preston who saved her."

"He came by earlier and told me the entire story. The event was a double blessing. He saved the woman, and he seems to have been cured of his fear of water."

He walked beside her as she continued toward the cottage. They stepped inside and she wrapped her arms around him and pressed her face to his chest. "I'm glad you came. I had a difficult time with Pres."

He leaned back and looked down at her, concern radiating from his face. "What happened?"

Tears stung the corners of her eyes. "He claims he's not had a drink for two weeks and that he'll never drink again. I know it takes more time than that, and another disappointment may lead him to find solace in whisky. He said he wants me back."

His eyes widened. "Doesn't he know we're seriously seeing each other?"

"I told him as much, but that didn't stop him from trying to get me to change my mind. He suggested we elope and take a trip around the world." Her lower lip trembled. "Without warning, he grabbed me and kissed me way too hard. His hands started roving and I had to work to get out of his embrace. It scared me, Nate."

His face reddened. "How far did he rove?"

"I got away before he did anything inappropriate."

"Did he hurt you?" His gaze went to her neck as if searching for bruising.

"No. Nothing like that. If he didn't know Mama was upstairs, I don't know how much further he might have forced himself on me. He's always been passionate, but never to that extreme."

He drew her against his chest. "I was planning on proposing to you at Christmas for a spring or summer wedding, but I think we should marry as soon as possible."

CHAPTER THIRTY

Nate heard himself say the words, but he couldn't believe he said them. Nor, by the look on Maureen's face, could she. "If you need time to think—"

"I love the idea."

He blinked. "You do?"

She nodded. "I love you so much, Nate, and I hate having to send you on your way every night. I hope to start at the Evanston nursing school in January. That would give us a few weeks together before that happens."

"I've been looking for a house to buy that has room for my medical practice too. There aren't any like that available. I wanted that in place first."

"We can start out in the cottage and move when we find a suitable house."

He frowned. "I'd feel funny not paying for our home."

"Then we'll talk to Da and arrange for us to rent from him. It would only be temporary."

He was warming to the idea. "You won't mind not living on the lake anymore?"

She kissed him. "Not if I can wake up with you beside me every morning."

He smiled at the thought and hugged her to him. "Would Christmas be too soon for you to plan the wedding? I know these things take planning."

She grinned. "I'd love it. I'm not sure how my parents will feel, but I don't need a big fancy wedding. A small one in the big house on Christmas Eve and then the day after Christmas we can honeymoon."

Thoughts whirled in his mind faster than a child's top. He had to rein in his emotions. Marrying Maureen was all he wanted, but small or large, all weddings required preparation time.

He took her by the hand and led her to the parlor where they sat side by side on the sofa. "Let's start at the beginning. You plan to apply to the nursing school in Evanston."

"Yes, and if I go there, I can stay with Aunt Callie during the week and come home to you every weekend." She snuggled up to him and brought her lips to his in a tender kiss.

What a blessed man he was to have such a wonderful woman who would soon be his wife. Was this really happening?

They parted and he pressed his forehead to hers. "Christmas is little more than a month away, but it seems like a year right now."

She chuckled. "I can already hear Mama saying there's not enough time to plan a proper wedding. I'm thinking maybe in front of the Christmas tree by the living room windows overlooking the lake. There's enough room with the parlor and living room opened to each other, and we'll keep it to family and close friends. Maybe later we can have a big celebration on the lawn when it warms up."

He stood, then pulled her to her feet, and kissed her. "I hate to get engaged and run, but I have appointments at the office this afternoon. Let's not tell your parents until tonight. Can you hold it in that long?"

She giggled. "I don't know. I want to bust out in song and shout the news to the world. But I'll be good."

An hour later, Maureen found her mother working on a needlepoint in the parlor. "Mama, I want to tell you something that should probably wait until tonight, but I'm about to burst."

Mama set her sewing aside. "Well, your mood has changed since the last time I saw you. Please sit." She patted the sofa cushion next to her.

She scooted over and sat. "Nate came by right after I left you."

"I saw his carriage in the circle. That was good timing."

Maureen pressed her lips together. She had agreed not to say anything about their engagement until tonight, and it wasn't right to break that promise. "After what happened with Preston today, I'm absolutely certain Nate is the man for me. I love him so much."

Mama laughed. "I've known that for weeks."

"I've known it for a while too, but never actually said it out loud until today when we both told each other, "I love you."

Mama wrapped Maureen in a hug. "That's a wonderful feeling the first time you hear those words." She leaned back and looked Maureen in the eyes. "Maybe you'll be getting a proposal and ring for Christmas."

If you only knew. She grinned, "Maybe so. I'm going to the cottage to fill out the nursing school application. I'll see you at dinner." She left the room with Mama calling out behind her, "He'd better not take too long. It takes time to plan a wedding."

Maureen greeted Nate at the door and welcomed his kiss, loving how the shift in their status had propelled them into a new level of tenderness. She took his hand and began to lead him into the dining room where the family had already gathered. He held her back. "Not yet. Get your coat."

"But they're waiting on us for dinner."

"Your dad knows we're taking a detour."

Puzzled, she walked over to the hall tree and lifted her wool coat from its hook. He couldn't have purchased a ring already. He had patients to see all afternoon.

He helped her into her wrap, and they walked hand in hand through the veranda and down the grassy slope to the lake. She glanced at the night sky. "Nate, have you ever seen so many stars?"

He wrapped her in his arms. "There are a lot aren't there? And He knows each of them and calls them by name. Come on, we don't want to keep the family waiting."

They continued walking. "Whatever it is we're about to do, why do we need to walk so far?"

"You'll see."

They came up on the Oak tree she'd come to dub "their tree" and he pulled her beneath the branches. "Not quite as secluded as it was before the leaves fell, but I still like this spot. It's perfect to do this." He dropped to a knee and took her left hand. "Maureen Quinn, I love you more than you can ever know. Will you marry me?"

She wished he could see the smile on her face. It had to be as large as the moon. "Yes. I'll marry you, Nate Murphy."

He slid a ring onto her finger then stood and gathered her in his arms and kissed her soundly. "Do you know of a justice of the peace where we can get it done tonight?"

She leaned back. "Are you serious?"

He chuckled. "No. If we did that your mother would shoot me. But it was a nice thought." They stayed wrapped in each other's arms, no talking, just loving being together in their private moment. He released her. "You don't have those fancy shoes on, do you?"

"No. Why?"

"Let's make a run for the house." He grabbed her hand, and they ran down the path and up the grassy slope, laughing and huffing and puffing. They reached the veranda and scrambled up the steps.

The whole family stood there.

"We heard you two all the way inside," Mama said. "What in the world is going on?"

Nate picked Maureen up and whirled her around. "She said yes, and we can't wait for Christmas."

He set Maureen down, and she held out her left hand. "I haven't been able to see the ring yet. I need some light."

They all moved indoors, and Maureen scooted over to a lamp and held out her hand. She stared at the solitaire diamond set on a gold band. "Oh, Nate I love it. But how? I mean you worked all afternoon, didn't you?"

He came up next to her and wrapped an arm around her waist. "It's my grandmother Murphy's ring. It was my mother's engagement ring, and she gave it to me before she died and said I was to save it for the woman God had for me.

The others came over, and Da took her in his arms. "I was thrilled when Nate called me this afternoon to ask my permission to propose."

Maureen stared at her fiancé. "You told Da? I almost told Mama but didn't. I thought we were going to tell them together."

"I couldn't propose without speaking with your father. I would have preferred asking in person, but the telephone had to do if I was going to give you the ring tonight."

"I have one question." Mama spoke up. "What did you mean before about Christmas?"

Maureen caught Nate's eye, and she nodded. He nodded at her then mouthed "Say it together?"

She nodded and grinned.

He counted to three on his fingers and they spoke at the same time. "That's when we want to get married."

EPILOGUE

Christmas Eve Day

Maureen stood before the mirror in the cottage bedroom that she and Nate would share, starting tomorrow night. He'd booked a suite on the top floor at the Whiting Hotel for tonight. They still hadn't located a home for them and his practice, but one on Main Street had recently come available and Nate was working on the details. If they bought it, it would be a couple of months more before they move in since the area to be used for the medical office would need to be rebuilt for that purpose.

Katie arranged a sprig of red flowers and baby's breath in Maureen's hair, then pinned her veil onto the crown of curls on her head. "I'm glad you aren't insisting on wearing a scarf like you did during my wedding."

She snickered. "It all seems so silly now, but at the time, it was the only thing that gave me confidence." She smiled. "That and Nate."

"I think he had already fallen in love with you by then. It was written all over his face."

"I know. God really has blessed me with him. I only hope I can be as much of a blessing to Nate as he is to me."

"You already are. You are the prettiest bride, Mo."

Maureen grinned and turned. "Not as pretty as you were."

Katie laughed. "I disagree, and there's a bridegroom waiting over at the big house whom I know would disagree with you as well.

Maureen smoothed the edges of the lacy yoke on her gown. "Do you think he'll like my dress?"

"How could he not? But if you came down the aisle wearing a gunny sack, he'd think you are beautiful. He adores you."

"And I adore him. I can't believe that a short time from now, I'll be Maureen Murphy. A married woman."

Katie grinned. "With all this adoring going on, how are you going to stand being apart during the week while you're at nursing school? I know I couldn't do it with Jake."

"It won't be easy, but I'll be home on weekends, and he'll take a day off once in a while and come down to Evanston for the day. I also get a month off in summer. It's only for a year."

A knock came at the open door, and Mama stepped into the room wearing a lace and silk gown the color of champagne. She embraced Maureen. "You are beautiful, my dear daughter, and you know we love Nate as if he were our own son. She stepped back and handed her a yellowed envelope.

Maureen stared at it. "Is this the something old I'm supposed to have?"

Mama smiled. "The old is the locket I wore at my own wedding that you're wearing. Back in 1871, when we evacuated from our home in Chicago the night of the fire, I found this envelope in my father's study and took it, intending to give it to him later. After we were safe in Lake Geneva, I decided to keep the thousand dollars that's in this envelope in case I needed it to help me to escape from the arranged marriage. I tucked it away in the trunk I'd brought with me the night of the fire.

"By the time the arranged marriage was canceled, I was caught up in planning my wedding to your Da, and crazy as it sounds, given its sizable amount, I forgot about the money. A few weeks ago, I was going through that old trunk and found the envelope. I want you and Nate to have it as my wedding gift. I know your granddaddy would want you to have it. Perhaps it will help Nate get that property he's looking at remodeled for his new office."

Maureen lifted the envelope flap and stared at the ten one-hundred-dollar bills. That's a lot of money. You're going to make me cry."

Katie produced a handkerchief and handed it to Maureen. "We can't let that happen."

A sudden realization came over her. Perhaps Mama should have given it to her without Katie being there. How must her sister feel? She looked at Katie. "We should share this. You only got married a few months ago and you'll be having a new mouth to feed soon."

Katie patted her still-flat tummy. "I might be tempted if it would buy something to stop my morning sickness. But, absolutely not. Little Junior will be well taken care of."

Da stepped into the room. "What's going on? All three of my favorite ladies are crying. This is supposed to be a happy day."

Maureen laughed and held up the envelope. "Mama just gave this to me." He smiled at Mama. "I'm glad you decided to give it to them, Anna." He faced Maureen and ran his gaze from the top of her head to her lace-trimmed hem. He pulled a handkerchief from his pocket and wiped his eyes. "Now I'm joining the rest of you. Maureen, you are a beautiful bride. My baby girl all grown up." He glanced at the clock on the dresser. "The time has come and your groom awaits you."

Maureen stepped over to the dresser and put the envelope in the top drawer. Then slipped on her white furry jacket. "I'm ready if you are."

"Let's go Katie." Mama scooted to the door with Katie trailing behind. Maureen slid her hand around Da's offered arm and they headed for the door.

They stepped outside the cottage and into softly falling snow. "We didn't need that today of all days," Da said.

Maureen glanced up at him. "Oh no. I love this It's very romantic."

"What if it snows so bad you and Nate can't get to your hotel tonight?"

"Then we'll stay in the cottage. Snowbound in a cozy cottage on our honeymoon sounds wonderful."

"Snowbound and not alone with your family next door."

"No worries. We'll make sure the door is locked."

Da laughed. "If that happens we'll leave you alone, at least for one night."

A short time later the string quartet, sitting beside the Christmas tree, started playing a Bach melody as her sisters stepped into the parlor from the hall and walked down the aisle. The pocket doors closed, and her grip on Da's arm tightened. He smiled down at her. The music paused and he winked. "There's our cue." Alice and Sophie stood at either side of the doors, their hands on the door pulls. Da nodded to them and the doors slid open. Every person in both the parlor and the adjacent living room stood.

The quartet began playing Pachelbel's *Canon in D major*, and Maureen and Da walked to the beginning of the aisle and turned to face the front. Every eye was on her but her gaze was on Nate, standing next to the large Christmas tree. His heart-stopping smile rivaled the lights on the tree and butterflies erupted in her stomach. The moment she'd dreamed of since they shared their first kiss was finally here. She held Nate's gaze, barely noticing who was sitting on either side of the narrow aisle as she and Da proceeded toward her groom.

Nate took a step forward and they came to a stop. Pastor Olsen asked, "Who gives this woman to be married to this man."

"Her mother and I do." Da took her hand and placed it in Nate's. "Take good care of my girl, Nate."

He nodded. "You know I will."

After the half-hour ceremony of music, the pastoral charge and vows, the pastor pronounced them married and told Nate he could kiss his bride. He tenderly leaned in and kissed her, letting it linger several seconds. He lifted his head and whispered, "I love you," The quartet started playing Vivaldi's *Four Seasons Spring* and Katie and Jake, who was the best man, marched out together followed by Maureen and Nate.

In the hall, Nate wrapped her in a hug and kissed her. "We did it, Mrs. Murphy."

She grinned up at him. "I love being called that."

They kissed again.

"Hey you two, you'll have plenty of time later for kissing. We need to be up front to receive the guests."

Maureen face Da. "If we must." She burst out laughing. "We're coming."

The family formed a reception line next to the Christmas tree and as Maureen turned to receive the first guest, her mouth almost fell open. Clean shaven, hair trimmed and combed, Preston smiled at her. "I seem to be making a habit of declining a Quinn wedding invitation then showing up anyway. "But I thought it appropriate that I wish you two well."

She accepted his offered hand. "Of course, we don't mind, Pres. How are you doing?"

"I'm doing well. I'm working for Mate, helping to build boats, and as soon as the ice melts, I'll be working for the cruise line on that job they offered."

"No more nightmares?"

"Once in a while, but thanks to your husband's referral to a specialist in the city, I've learned how to cope." He leaned in and loosely embraced her, then shook hands with Nate. "You take good care of her."

Nate grinned. "No need to worry, my friend. Glad to hear the methods you learned are helping."

Pres headed for the hall, not stopping to mingle with the guests.

"I guess that's all he wanted. Any regrets?"

Maureen looked up at her husband. "You are the one God chose for me, and I'm right where I want to be."

He leaned down and kissed her. "Well said, Mrs. Murphy."

A NOTE FROM THE AUTHOR

One of the things I've enjoyed about writing these historical novels set in my hometown of Lake Geneva, Wisconsin is all the new and fascinating things I learn about the history of the area.

As noted in the Acknowledgments, I wouldn't have the depth of resources to pull from without the Geneva Lake Museum and the Lake Geneva Public Library. The first place I head when beginning to research is the microfilms of the local newspaper from the period my story is taking place. I often find mentions of events that took place then that I can work into the storyline.

One event in this story is the capsizing of the steam yacht *Celerity*. The name of the boat is fictitious but, thanks to an offhand remark made by someone at the museum, I was drawn to a microfilm of a newspaper story about a steam yacht called *Dispatch* that sunk in Geneva Lake during a wild storm. Since that sinking occurred a year later than the one in my book, I couldn't use the specific event, but I did include how a woman was saved from drowning by her mutton sleeves that served as life preservers. Like the saying goes, you can't make this stuff up. This was one of those.

I didn't know much about the Columbian Exposition of 1893, but when I realized it took place the same year as my story, I had to include it. I'd purchased the book *The Devil in White City* years ago but had never read it. It tells of two parallel events that occurred back then, the building of the World's Fair site where Jackson Park is now and how the city was terrorized during that time by a serial killer. I only make a short mention of the serial killer in my story, but the book was a valuable resource to me in learning about the fair and its attractions, most especially the Ferris wheel.

I also learned how the country was coming to the end of a smallpox epidemic when the fair opened. Because of the influx of people from all over the world, attendees were warned to be very careful about germs and to wash their hands a lot. Of course, back then people weren't as well educated as today about such things, and the fair sprouted a smallpox epidemic of its own. As brought out in the story, the vaccine was already available, but people were slow to take it seriously. Of course, having Maureen come down with the virus worked perfectly in bringing her and Doctor Nate Murphy together.

We hear a lot about Post Traumatic Stress Disorder (PTSD) today, but in 1893 they didn't know much about it except for what they called shell shock. Shell shock, which is PTSD, was recognized as a condition many Civil War soldiers experienced after being exposed to loud cannons and gun sounds over a sustained length of time. I first learned about PTSD and its symptoms when I wrote a contemporary novella about a wounded warrior who had lost his leg in Afghanistan. I didn't intend for Preston to have PTSD when I first began writing Shelter Bay, but I soon realized as I wrote his personality changes and fear of water was precisely that. I began writing his mood swings fears to fit that of a PTSD victim. If you want to know more about PTSD, search for it on the internet and you'll find a ton of information.

As I write this, I'm preparing to write book three in the series, Tranquility Point. It takes place during World War I, and I'm learning a lot about home front Lake Geneva during that time. It's scheduled to for release in the spring of 2020.

Until then, happy reading and God bless!

Pam

ABOUT THE AUTHOR

Pamela has written most of her life, beginning with her first diary at age eight. Her novels include *Thyme For Love, Surprised by Love in Lake Geneva, Wisconsin (a reissue of Love Finds You in Lake Geneva, Wisconsin)*, a 1933 historical romance set in her hometown, and *Second Chance Love*, a contemporary romance set at a rodeo in rural Illinois. Her novella, *What Lies Ahead*, is included in *The Bucket List Dare* collection, and another novella, *If These Walls Could Talk*, was published in May 2017, in a collection called *Coming Home: A Tiny House Collection*. Future novels include *Whatever is True*, a sequel to Second Chance Love.

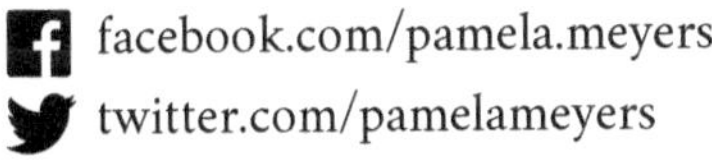

facebook.com/pamela.meyers
twitter.com/pamelameyers

Safe Refuge

Newport of the West—Book One

In two days, wealthy Chicagoan, Anna Hartwell, will wed a man she loathes. She would refuse this arranged marriage to Lyman Millard, but the Bible clearly says she is to honor her parents, and Anna would do most anything to please her father–even leaving her teaching job at a mission school and marrying a man she doesn't love.

The Great Chicago Fire erupts, and Anna and her family escape with only the clothes on their backs and the wedding postponed. Father moves the family to Lake Geneva, Wisconsin, where Anna reconnects with Rory Quinn, a handsome immigrant who worked at the mission school. Realizing she is in love with Rory, Anna prepares to break the marriage arrangement with Lyman until she learns a dark family secret that changes her life forever.

Tranquility Point

Newport of the West—Book Three

Hannah Murphy is determined to make the summer of 1916, the best it can be before she heads off to law school in the fall. Like her mother and grandmother before her, she is inclined to "break the mold" when it comes to societal expectations of a young woman of means. Her mother was the first woman in town to wear bloomers, and Hannah becomes the first to ditch swim dresses in favor of a practical swimsuit that allows freedom to move through the water.

At the first gathering of the summer, she reacquaints with tall, handsome Ted Bauer, also an aspiring attorney. Ted, who is of German descent, had a huge crush on Hannah when he was in eighth grade, and she was in sixth. He's no longer the gangly boy she remembers and is quite appealing. With Geneva Lake as their backdrop, their summer romance escalates, until the dark cloud of the Great War can no longer be ignored. Although the U.S. has not yet joined the fray, people of German descent are seen with mistrust, and Ted enlists with the British Army to take the heat of discrimination off his family. With the future on hold, Hannah bids her fiancé farewell as he goes to war. Only God knows if she will ever see him again or if they will ever be able to recapture what they had those few short summer months.

Coming from Pamela S. Meyers in May 2021:

Rose Harbor

Book Four of the Newport of the West series.

Stay up-to-date on your favorite books and authors with our free e-newsletters.

ScriveningsPress.com

9 781649 170163